HOUSE OF TERRORS

AN ANTHOLOGY OF FEAR

EDITED BY
ANTHONY GIANGREGORIO

**NOW AVAILABLE FROM
UNDEAD PRESS**

ZOMBIE TALES: AN UNDEAD ANTHOLOGY
DEADLY HUNT: A ZOMBIE SURVIVAL STORY
VICTORY OF THE DEAD: A ZOMBIE NOVEL
THE FALL OF PITTSBURGH: A ZOMBIE NOVEL
ZOMBIE KILL: PREDATOR OR PREY?
THE DAY THE WORLD DIED: A ZOMBIE STORY
AN UNDEAD CHRISTMAS: A ZOMBIE ANTHOLOGY

Copyright © 2012 Undead Press
ISBN Softcover ISBN 13: 978-1-61199-062-1
ISBN 10: 1-611990-62-9
All rights reserved.
Undead Press is an imprint of Living Dead Press.
ww.livingdeadpress.com
All stories contained within this book have been published with permission from the authors.
No part of this book may be reproduced or transmitted in any form or by any means, electronic or mechanical, including photocopying, recording, or by any information storage and retrieval system, without permission in writing from the copyright owner.
This is a work of fiction.
Names, characters, places and incidents either are the product of the author's imagination or are used fictitiously, and any resemblance to any actual persons, living or dead, events, or locales is entirely coincidental. This book was printed in the United States of America.
For more info on obtaining additional copies of this book, go to:
www.undeadpress.com

Table of Contents

FACE TIME

ANTHONY GIANGREGORIO

"Wake up, buddy. Rise and shine."

The words were barely heard. They sounded as if his ears were underwater.

"Come on, I need you to wake up," the voice said.

His memory was fuzzy and at first he didn't even know his own name, but then, slowly, it came back.

Frank Parsons.

Yes, that was his name, he was positive.

A second later, he realized he was sitting up, in a chair to be precise. He wanted to rub his face, to take the grogginess away, but when he tried to move his right arm, it didn't budge. He tried again with the same result.

Bright white light struck him in the face and he screamed. He tried to blink but the light wouldn't stop and he wondered if his eyelids had been somehow taped open like he'd seen in movies when the person in the chair had to see something and couldn't be allowed to look away.

He was so groggy, fuzzy even. It felt like he had a hangover, but he didn't remember drinking that hard the night before. Come to think of it, he didn't remember much of anything before this exact moment.

"What…what's going on, where am I?" Frank said, his voice barely a whisper. His mouth felt like he'd been gargling sand, as did his throat. Come to think of it, his face burned, like he'd been out in the sun for far too long.

"What's it look like, Frank? Where do you think you are?"

Frank considered the question, the owner of the voice was hidden behind the bright white light.

"Uhm, I don't know exactly. I remember going to Ramona's Bar and Grille and then a hot-looking woman came over and bought me a drink. Then she bought me a few more." He paused as he gathered his thoughts, his memories a jumble of images. "Then I went to the bathroom and…"

"And that's when she slipped two valiums into your drink," the voice said. The bright light was suddenly dimmed slightly, and though Frank couldn't blink, he was able to see better as the white spots faded from his vision. The owner of the voice was still hidden behind the now dimmed but still strong light, but what he held before him, even with Frank's memory lapse, was all too clear.

"Do you know what this is, Frank?"

Frank stared at the object in the man's hand. He could tell his captor was a man by the deep voice and the muscled arm the hand belonged to; the hand holding something that had to be a joke.

"Come on, sure you do. What's it look like if you had to guess?"

Frank said nothing and the item was pushed closer.

"Tell me, Frank, or else."

The threat was all too clear and Frank had a good feeling that the threat wasn't an idle one. But still he remained silent, for to say what he thought the item was could only mean one thing. One terrible, unimaginable thing.

"I know you know what this is, Frank," the man said as he shook the item from side to side. "You recognize the scar on the left cheek, don't you? No? How 'bout the thin mustache?"

Frank said nothing, the horror overwhelming him.

"Fine, then if you need more proof that this is what you think it is, here you go." The man raised a small mirror even with Frank's face, and as it became level with Frank and he saw his visage,

Frank opened his mouth and screamed and shrieked and begged God to save him.

For before him, instead of the pink face he knew so well, was nothing but a red mass of oozing blood, under muscles and tendons that made up his face. Now he knew why his face stung so bad, for the nerve endings were exposed to the air.

He had no fucking face!

He struggled to get free but it was to no avail, and as the man watched Frank squirm and scream and moan, he smiled in pleasure.

Vengeance was so sweet sometimes.

When Frank finally stopped screaming, his sobs now soft and barely audible, his head sunk low to his chest, the man tossed the skinned face onto Frank's lap. It laid there, like a rubber mask, gazing up at Frank accusingly.

"Don't worry, Frank, I can see you're upset about this whole thing. So I tell you what…" The man reached over and picked up a box of three inch nails and a hammer.

"I'll put it back on for you."

As the man got to work, Frank began to scream even louder.

THE PROTECTOR

DANIEL LOUBIER

I stand in front of the house, on the sidewalk, staring at the old abandoned colonial, tucked away by itself in the cul-de-sac at the end of my street. It's nighttime, past curfew, so there's no chance of me being seen. I know the horror that lays in wait inside the walls of the old house and my body goes rigid as I recall details from my last visit. I've been inside before, but it never gets any easier.

The house is long deserted; nobody's lived there for some time now. Funny, save for a few minor cosmetic issues, there's nothing immediately creepy about the house, at least not from the outside. The white paint is clean with no chipping; the foundation reveals no cracks and the wood isn't riddled with termite holes. But the lawn is overgrown, the tall grass and weeds keepers of the trash and debris that float by on a windy day. A shutter on the window to the right of the front door hangs loosely from a single hinge, the window behind it shattered, the result of an altercation, perhaps. Other than that, the house remains perfectly intact.

The inside of the house presents an entirely different atmosphere. My older brother used to say the place is haunted, even when the previous owners, the Stiles, still lived here. He claimed to have seen ghosts on occasion, looking down on him from the windows upstairs. I'd tell him he was full of it.

When the Stiles weren't around, he'd dare me to go inside but I never would. I was always too afraid I'd find out that he was right.

A metallic *squeee* pinches the air as I push open the wooden gate which still stands firm after all the months that have passed since the Day of Infection. It's been close to two years now. So many lives were lost. Friends, family members, so many torn apart by the vicious disease that turned people into raging maniacs with no purpose other than to destroy and devour all who were unlike them.

It was insane at first. Nobody knew what happened. One day people just…flipped. Went berserk. Even the so-called 'scientists' can't explain what triggered the sudden and frenzied behavior. Some claim a parasite in the drinking water was the source of it all. Others claim it was due to a bad vaccine batch. But nobody knew. Nobody knows. The only certainty is that it doesn't seem to be coming to an end any time soon.

I step inside the gate, close it behind me, and turn to face the house. I steel myself against the gate, and prepare myself for what I'm about to see. I proceed to step down the walk. The leaves and weeds that grow up through the cracks fall under my feet as silent and lifeless as the air around me.

When the experts determined that the disease was being further spread by bites, people started to build borders around many of the neighborhoods—mine included—in order to keep out the infected. They started with a tall, chain-link fence, which helped for a while, but when the zombies figured out a way to climb over the top, people started using those concrete jersey barriers used on highways. They lined them all along the fence and then stacked them about ten feet high. With no footholds or handholds to grab onto, the zombies were unable to climb over.

Anyone who was infected and had somehow remained inside the border, was quickly disposed of and tossed over the wall, left to remain on the land between neighborhoods—the Deadlands. We haven't had one go rogue in about six months. No intruders. No unwelcome guests. And yet, our peaceful little society is still tearing apart at the seams. Some realize it, but most neither care to acknowledge nor repair. There's so much unrest. People are tired of being locked up inside the concrete walls. Some have even taken to using ladders to climb over the border, to escape in search of a better way of life in another neighborhood.

Sometimes they come back, sometimes they don't. We only hope that the ones who don't have managed to find a better situation for themselves.

I continue to approach the old house. A breeze rolls through the trees and tousles my hair, carrying with it a *sshh*, as if begging me to remain quiet and still so as not to disturb the evil that resides within the home.

My friends know that there is something in there. Well, they think they know, but they're not actually *aware* that they know. Each of them claims to have witnessed a person walking around, or rather, staggering around.

They all provide different descriptions of what this person looks like. One says tall, another says short. One says long hair, one says curly, another says bald. They really don't know for sure.

However, they are one hundred percent correct. There is a zombie inside the house. I've seen it before. I've touched it. It wants to bite me but I'm too quick and I leave before it's able to get a nibble.

I told my parents I'm staying at Jimmy's house tonight. I told them we're going to stay up and have a horror movie marathon. They like Jimmy. They never give me any crap about hanging around with him. Then there's Tommy. Let's just say this lie wouldn't work if I said I was hanging out with Tommy. He's a bit of a brat and kind of a show-off, but he's still my friend.

I'm at the porch now, standing at the foot of the stairs.

I take the first step.

I look to my left, into the window next to the door. I don't see it. Hmm.

I take another step. I check the window again. I can see a lot of the front room now. I see the couch, the TV stand, and the carpet. But the zombie isn't there. Interesting.

I continue up the steps until I'm standing on the front porch. Nervously, I take a look around, behind me, out into the street, at the houses across the way.

Lights are on and I can barely make out a TV showing in someone's living room. But no one's watching. No one knows I'm here. I turn back to the house and slowly walk over to the window.

I look inside.

There's no sign of the zombie. This is very good. If I can't see it from the front porch, then the rest of the town definitely won't be able to see it from the street. I walk to the door and reach for the doorknob.

Do I really want to do this? Do I really need to see this?

Of course I do. It's the only way.

I turn the knob—it's unlocked—and push the door open.

The house looks just the same as it did yesterday. Nothing is out of place. Nothing is missing. There are no other zombies, which is another good sign. It's also a good sign that I didn't hear the chains clanking in the kitchen when I opened the door.

I walk left of the center staircase, across the blood-stained carpet of the living room and toward the kitchen.

I pause when I reach the doorway between rooms. By my estimation, the zombie should be just around the corner, to my right, either sitting on the floor or standing against the wall. My heart is now thumping.

Even in the darkness, I'm sure my shirt is puffing out with every beat. I nervously rub my index fingers against my thumbnails as I try to force myself over the threshold.

You wanted to come here. You're supposed to come here.

In that moment I recall the first time I saw a zombie up close. My brother had taken me to see it. He'd brought me out into the Deadlands one day.

We used a ladder and climbed over the wall.

It was terrifying.

Jake told me he'd seen one while he was out on the other side of the border one night. He said he wanted me to come see it. I was hesitant at first. Too scared, just like always. But eventually, he convinced me it was harmless. He said it hadn't eaten flesh in so long and that it was close to dying, so it barely had any energy left. He said it wouldn't try to bite us because it didn't even have enough strength to close its mouth. I still didn't want to go because the threat of being seen by other zombies remained. Again, my brother claimed there were hardly any out there. So, I went with him.

We got an early start, just after sunrise. Most people were still asleep at that time. After all, there were no jobs to perform, no professions to drive off to. These days, people just stay at home and try to live each day the best they can, given the circumstances.

We took Dad's ladder, set it against the wall, and made for the Deadlands in search of a zombie.

Jake knew where it was so it didn't take long to find it, maybe a couple hours. It was just lying there, under a tree. We approached it cautiously, until we were only a few feet away.

I'd never gotten that close to one before. Its skin had that same grayish pallor, just like the rest of them. But it seemed very tired. The eyes looked pale, watery and lifeless, even more so than a zombie's eyes normally look. When our shadows cast over its head, it looked up at us, acknowledging our presence. Its mouth was open but my brother was right, it had barely enough strength to pick up its head. It remained slack-jawed until its head came to rest again on the ground. It was the eeriest thing I'd ever seen.

I've been standing in the doorway between the living room and the kitchen for ten minutes now. For some reason, I always hesitate when I reach this point. I know I must continue, but there's a part of me that doesn't want to see. But then I remember why I'm here, and I remember my promise. I take a long breath and slowly exhale, quietly, so as not to alarm the zombie.

I walk into the kitchen.

It's on the floor. Its gaze is flat, staring across the kitchen at nothing. Drool, pus and mucous flow through its rotting teeth, over torn, chapped lips. It feels my presence and looks up at me. Milky eyes stare into mine. Gray, loose skin is rotting away from the body. The zombie is missing some hair, too. It must have ripped it out or something since the last time I was here. Otherwise, not much has changed.

But it doesn't get any easier.

It's in the same clothes it's been wearing for three months now.

"Hello, Jake," I say to him.

He only stares back at me. Violence, desire, and hunger in his eyes. I wonder if he remembers me coming back all these nights.

"How are you tonight?" I ask. I know he can't answer, but it's the idle chat I make with myself that helps me remember he was once human and might still be. God he looks awful; cold, dead and wanting to tear my flesh from my bones. I can't help but stare and think of how big a mistake it was, heading off into the Deadlands that day.

My brother wanted so badly to show me the zombie. I wanted nothing to do with it. He kept saying how 'cool' it was to see a zombie up close. After all, he'd already seen it once. Admittedly, and though I was still scared, I thought it might be cool as well. Plus, it seemed highly unlikely that either of us would get hurt.

When my brother started poking at it with a stick, the zombie really seemed to get agitated. I asked Jake to stop but he kept laughing as he poked at it again and again. The zombie grunted and moaned, even tried to roll over, away from my brother, but Jake continued to antagonize the poor thing.

At one point—and I don't know how neither of us saw it happen—the zombie must have found the very last bit of rage inside itself. It lunged and bit my brother's leg. It was barely a scratch, hardly a nip, but it was enough. We both knew my brother would eventually turn into one of them. We just didn't know how long it would take. I froze up. My brother, my personal hero, was going to turn into one of those *things*. Of course, always the hero, he told me not to worry. He said it was only a scratch and that he might not even turn. I knew he was lying. And I knew that he knew that I knew he was lying. We left all the rest unspoken.

He then said to me, "Let's wait until dark before we climb back over the border. If I'm still alive, you can take me to the Stiles' house and chain me up inside. Then you can visit me whenever you want and I won't be able to hurt you."

I cried like a little kid who'd just found out that Santa doesn't exist. I knew what he'd said was only meant to make me feel better, but truth be told, I felt like I'd just lost my best friend. I knew he wouldn't be the same. Even as a zombie, and even if I kept him 'alive,' he wouldn't be the real Jake. I cried until my throat was raw and my eyes swollen. My brother held me the entire time. He kept telling me I was going to be all right, that I would be safe.

When I think back on it now, I should have been the one holding him. I should have been the one telling him it would be all right and that soon he would be in a better place. But he was always the stronger one. He was always the one willing to swim into the deep end of the pool, or to stand toe-to-toe with the school bully. He was always the protector. But now, he wasn't going to be able to protect me anymore. Sadly, he soon wouldn't even be able to protect me from himself.

So many people had turned since the Day of Infection. So many families had loved ones who'd turned. All the while I kept thinking, *Not my family. That won't happen to us*. And just like that, it did.

In the end, I couldn't leave my brother out there in the Deadlands, walking among the undead, so I did like he asked and I chained him up in the house.

First, we waited hours for the sun to go down. When it was dark, we snuck back over the border, into the town and ran home. When we reached our house, I crawled into our basement alone and grabbed some chains and a padlock, then met my brother back outside. My parents never even knew I was there.

As we ran to the old house, he still seemed fine and for a minute, I actually started to think we might not have to lock him up, but he insisted. "Just in case," he said, so we ran to the house at the end of the street.

Once inside, we chatted for hours. We talked about who the prettiest girls were in the neighborhood and about what each of us would do if given a few minutes alone with any of them. We even played cards to pass the time. After a while, I actually started to feel better. I started to feel like this would all just blow over and he would be fine.

But around four o'clock in the morning, he started to change.

First, his breath started to smell like a dead animal. Then he complained of stomach pains. Soon after, he began vomiting blood. That's when he told me to leave. He didn't want me to see him change. He said he didn't want this moment to be my last memory of him when he was alive.

I stayed anyway, though I wanted to run so bad. I wanted to turn and sprint through the living room, out the door and down the steps and never see the Stiles' house again. For the first time in my life, I knew that I was now the one who would have to be strong. As much as he wanted me to leave, Jake needed me to be strong, and if I wasn't, well, that didn't leave anybody else.

So, for the first time in our lives, I was there for him. I kept my distance and watched him become one of them. I never cried so hard in my life as I did that night. I couldn't even talk to him. I tried, but words never touched my lips. It was torture, for both of us, but mostly for him. I tried to reach out for him a couple times, but he waved me back as he doubled over in pain, clutching his insides.

Then, after a few minutes, it was over. And just like that, he was no longer my brother. He was no longer Jake. Just a soulless body, inhabited now by something much darker, and much more evil. I whispered goodbye and ran out of the house. I didn't go back for weeks.

Now, I visit him every night. Occasionally I find a dead bird or a dead frog on the street, likely killed by a neighbor's dog or cat, and I give it to him to eat. It's enough to sustain him, but I don't know for how long.

"I miss you, bro." I reach out a hand to touch his head. Just to feel his hair, his face, to see if there's any warmth left in his skin. He snaps at me, nearly bites my hand, but I pull it away quick. He gets on his feet, ready to take me. It's time to go.

"I love you, Jake. I'll see you tomorrow, okay?"

He stares at me, death swirling around inside his opaque eyes and a low growl bubbling from his quivering mouth.

I turn and walk out of the kitchen, through the living room, and to the front door. I wipe my eyes with my sleeve. This is hell. I just want to go back to that day and tell him, "No, I don't want to see a zombie up close." But I can't reverse what's happened. What's done is done and it's time for me to leave.

I glance back to see if he's standing in the doorway to the kitchen, watching me, but there's nobody there. Perhaps he's sitting down on the floor again. Or maybe he's still standing there, staring at the space I occupied only seconds ago. It doesn't matter. I'll be back tomorrow night. I always come back. Because he's my brother, and I'll always love him for who he was. Zombie or not, he's still my blood, even if the heart doesn't pump anymore.

I walk outside onto the porch, down the steps and onto the walk. I look up. It's a full moon tonight. It's bright enough outside to see all the way down to the other end of the street. If anyone saw me, they'd surely ask what I was up to. Hell, if anyone knew about my brother, they'd put a bullet in his head.

He's my secret now. Even my parents don't know, and I'm not quite sure what they would do if they ever found out about him. They'd probably cry, much like they did when they found out he'd, *left the neighborhood,*' but it would probably be much worse. I don't think my mother could bear the knowledge that one of her sons was a zombie, and my dad was inconsolable after losing his first-born son.

So I keep it to myself. I have to. My brother was the strong one, but now he's gone. So that just leaves me.

The protector.

TIME TO SCREAM

SHANE KOCH

The still-barking canine manifestation of the dreaded Viking Prince Gourde Heflin was finished, locked in place by the Sorrow Equation.

Stella stumbled up the basement stairs while tripping over twitching corpses; she spared one look back at the four-legged tyrant. The dog despondently howled at the runic equation Stella had scrawled with the blood of the priests, his glowing eyes mesmerized by the mathematical misery dripping down the pulsating concrete wall.

She thanked God again for Richard and his arcane algebra; his sacrifice had saved her, if only for a moment. She didn't know how long the bristling, snorting creature would be held in place by the ancient magic.

She finally understood why Richard made her memorize the strange math. He knew he was going to die, and he wanted her to live.

She considered her terrifying reality and laughed hysterically in an effort to calm her senses. She wished the evil dog in the basement a slow death for what it made Richard do to himself. She tried to wipe the visions from her mind, but the memories were too fresh, and she wished for a moment that she was dead so that she didn't have to remember.

Behind her eyes, she envisioned the slip-n-slide covered with razor blades and awash with Richard's blood; she shuddered and nearly lost control of her fragile sanity. She screamed in frustration. She knew she was broken—her soul was soiled in every way.

She would never be the same.

She had to get out of the house, had to get to the car, had to get away forever. Despite the complete rape of her being, she still wanted to live. Why? Because *fuck those fuckers*! Stella would be the last little thing that the monsters couldn't beat.

The stuffed moose head seemed to accuse her silently as she burst from the basement and into the hall, as did the assorted eyeballs of the household staff which rested in the crooks of the dead animal's antlers.

She couldn't bear to glance at the grotesque abstract one last time as she ran toward the front door, where the promise of sanity was just beyond her reach. She dared not look into the sitting room as she passed; a drying and fly-specked abattoir now, it was a ghastly remembrance of the grandparents and their children, a three-dimensional diorama of their forced chainsaw battle—just one of the installations in this museum of evil and desperation.

All the terrors of Horror House would ebb, she reasoned frantically, if she could just reach the exit.

Finally, she snatched her purse from the foyer table and clutched the front doorknob. The house shuddered and a seismic ripple tore through the structure, nearly knocking Stella from her feet.

The house, a malevolent being filled with life, tore itself apart. She jerked the front door open—all the while expecting an axe between her shoulder blades or a clammy hand to drag her back into hell—and flung herself outside. She ran as hard as she could down the long driveway, where her car waited for her.

Another inhuman screech filled the night and Stella looked back at Horror House. She screamed as her sanity ripped away from her brain in electric and bloody strips.

The house collapsed upon itself, a glass-shattering and wood-splintering origami, folded by the invisible hands of evil. The remains of the house twisted and transmogrified alchemically, changing shape and substance.

It condensed into a giant blood-red and crystalline snowflake bathed in black lightning, floating over an empty and smoking foundation. The snowflake smiled at her, and she knew that all the horrific suffering of the weekend was contained inside of it, fueling it, propelling its maniacal propensity to unleash unspeakable torments upon the innocent.

A hundred giant snakes with human heads rose from the smoke and chanted incantations to the snowflake, a serpentine chorus that swayed in the sparking flashes of the ebony arc-light. The clicking of their uncoiling, armored scales and the chittering of their prayer-spewing teeth was deafening.

From the oily smoke lumbered a beast whose appearance fucked and mutilated Stella's immortal soul with thrusting, grasping fear, driving away all but one quivering sliver of self-preserving reason.

The squid's comically huge white eyes stared at her hungrily, rolling and wet with anticipation. Its beak snapped like a gunshot, spattering viscous tendrils of ooze with every labored breath. Useless and broken batwings flapped atop its flabby, mottled gray head and its tentacles lashed out, smashing the driveway and throwing up rocks. Monstrously huge, hairy legs that twitched and trembled carried the beast along slowly. The unreal horror dragged a pulsing, vein-riddled black cord that was attached to something within the smoking foundation of Horror House. It reminded Stella of an umbilical cord.

The thing looked at Stella with one eye and the other popped, deflating with a gush of clear fluid. Three of the spider legs broke at once, giving the creature painful pause as the exoskeletal limbs cracked open and blew large, glistening slabs of crab-like meat into the air.

When the monster screeched in pain, it was a high-pitched dolphin wail that nearly burst Stella's eardrums. The creature was not meant for the world of man.

She turned and ran from the defective, self-destructing monstrosity, laughing as tears ran down her cheeks. The squid-thing laboriously forged on, intent on murder. It burst, broke, and leaked all the way, leaving a trail of itself behind; the black cord flopped in a wake of multicolored gore.

Stella settled into her car and slammed the door. She rummaged in her purse for her keys as the dying horror in the rearview mirror crawled ever closer.

With both hands, she frantically pulled fistfuls of nothing from her purse while she screamed for her keys to appear. A rain of make-up, receipts, credit cards, tissues, cotton balls, and everything but keys fell on the passenger seat.

The thing struggled closer, bleeding from every orifice, seeming to want to live just long enough to kill Stella. No keys! Richard always said that her cluttered purse would cause her problems one day, but she never figured it would kill her.

The monster died just before it reached her car. The behemoth shuddered once and perished from the world of the living. Stella watched in the rearview as the black umbilical cord pulled the creature's corpse back into the smoke and down into the foundation.

The chanting, human-headed snakes withdrew into darkness and the snowflake was gone in one final strike of bright, eye-searing lightning.

Her hands still searched for the keys as Stella realized it was finally over. The entire weekend of unimaginable torment was behind her.

She understood that she would never be able to live normally after the abominations she had witnessed. Her entire family had slaughtered themselves at the whim of an insane ghost. She stared blankly at herself in the rearview and noticed her hair had turned white.

The survivor didn't recognize the eyes staring back at her.

She dug for her keys again in the recesses of her deep purse. Something grabbed her hand and pulled. Her body disappeared in a flash of blue light that shattered the windows of her car. All that remained was her cluttered purse, flopped half empty under the steering wheel.

Stella found herself on a flat, black ashen plain. Clusters of dead trees dotted the horizon, and beyond them volcanoes belched smoke and fire into the starless, black skies.

Her clothes were gone and it was cold; a bone-chilling wind ripped across the ground and through her naked, shivering body. In the distance, Stella could hear the faint dolphin screeches of the squid creatures.

She looked in all directions and realized she was being approached from all sides. Children, a hundred of them, naked and bloody, were slowly walking toward her from everywhere, their feet shuffling through the ash.

They were all crying and carrying straight razors in their chubby little hands. The children called her Mommy.

Stella convulsed with uncontrollable laughter.

She laughed until it was time to scream.

OBSESSION

JULIE R. KENDRICK

You're so beautiful. I just want to run a knife down your cheek to slice your perfect skin. I want to see the blood run down your face and spill onto your perfect breasts. I wait for that day. I think it will be soon.

I remember the first time I saw you. It was in a bar and I was in my favorite corner, great for people watching. You walked in with another girl. She had short blonde hair and was overweight. Your beauty lit up the room.

You were wearing a black trouser suit with a pastel green blouse and smart black pumps. I saw your huge deep brown eyes, your perfect little nose and your cupid bow mouth, which was painted with a subtle peach lip gloss.

You swished your long dark hair and I instantly felt the connection. I know you did too because you looked over at me. I think you smiled. I felt warm in my stomach. That was the start of our relationship.

I was there the next week, too, in my usual spot, waiting for you. I waited for a long time and eventually there you were, with the same chubby blonde girl who served only to make your beauty more breathtaking.

This time you were wearing a navy skirt suit and a cream top. I could see your legs. You weren't wearing any pantyhose. I couldn't breathe properly for about five minutes, just at the thought of your legs.

I had to close my eyes and focus on my breathing. I was annoyed. I had missed a whole thirty seconds of gazing at your beauty. You didn't look at me that day. It was my fault for closing my eyes. I won't make that mistake again.

Why didn't you come the following week? I waited for you. Are you angry with me? You mustn't be. I punished myself for last week's error. I have the burn scars to prove it.

I found out your name today. Someone called out 'Emma' and you turned to look who it was.

They weren't calling you. I have to admit, I was a little disappointed. It doesn't do you justice. Emma is such a plain name, more suited to the fat girl you spend a lot of time with. I couldn't stay long today. I was upset with you, Emma. I don't like your name.

I'm so glad you came this week. I can't believe how silly I was last week when I found out your name, Emma. I wasted time and had to punish myself again when I got home.

The hospital said I was lucky I didn't sever my whole finger. I don't think all the feeling will come back but I don't care. You're worth it. My Emma.

I'm so happy. I followed you tonight. I know where you live. St. Mark's Avenue is perfect for you. Beautiful houses with long driveways. You have hedges. I hid in one and watched you through your window.

You made some toast. I saw you take off your jacket and you were wearing a low cut t-shirt. I could see the top of your breasts. My breathing went funny again but I didn't take my eyes off you. I have to confess, I got an erection. I soiled your hedge.

I'm sorry but nothing can spoil my happiness today, Emma. The day is fast approaching that we will meet and you'll be able to tell me how you feel about me. We can talk about our connection. I love you, Emma.

I have never been so angry. Who is he? Who the *hell* is he? How dare you betray me like this; showing up with him out of the blue. And *flirting* like a slut. Crossing and uncrossing your uncovered legs, acting like a whore.

He bought you drinks. Is that how he's paying for your time, whore? I couldn't even finish my drink. I had to leave before something happened. It can't happen in a public place. You laughed as I left.

Were you laughing at me? Just wait, Emma, slut, whore, cheap bitch. You won't laugh soon.

I'm sorry. I am so sorry. Please come back. Two weeks I've waited for you. I've been in the bar every day but you don't come. I've punished myself so much. You'll see. I have more scars just for you. I need my fingers so I cut my legs lots of times. I'll show you. I'm so sorry. Please, Emma, come back to me.

You came back. You had the obese girl with you. *He* wasn't there. You looked so sad. I didn't like it. Was it him who made your perfect mouth turn down at the corners?

Didn't he treat you with the respect you deserve? He's a stupid, stupid man, Emma. You may be sad now but I'll make you happy. We'll be together forever. Soon. The day is nearly here. Be patient, my sweet Emma.

I saw that man today. The one who made you sad. He won't be making you sad any more. He won't be making anyone sad any more. He bled on my sweater. I liked that sweater. It made me angrier. He bled more. You see, Emma? Look what I did for you. Can you feel our connection? It's so strong now. It's okay, darling, I won't let you wait much longer.

There was a policeman at my door today. He asked me questions about that man. The one that died. I said I didn't know anything.

The policeman went away but I think he'll be back. My head is hurting so much. I need to make you mine now. I will see you tomorrow, Emma.

It's such a peaceful feeling standing outside your front door, knowing you're inside, waiting for me. I savor the moment—the last moment of being alone. I wonder if you're looking in the mirror. I hope so.

You should commit your beautiful face to memory just like I have. I will always be able to see your huge brown eyes, your perfect little button nose, and your lips—your full peachy lips.

I'll remember running my hands through your silky dark hair. I'll remember the look in your eyes when I produce my knife and I will remember your sharp intake of breath just before I slice your flawless skin.

I'll remember the warmth of your blood flowing through my fingers, the wideness of your eyes as I bring the point of my blade close to your pupil. I'll remember the sound of your eyeball popping under the pressure.

I'll remember the life draining from you, your gift to me for the love I've given you.

My erection is painful now.

Your doorbell plays *Silent Night*.

It's fitting.

A DEATH IN THE FAMILY

SAMUEL J. GUSS

A funeral services student once told me in class that a funeral service served an important role in accepting the passing away of a loved one. It gave closure to the bereaved by allowing them to witness that their loved one was truly dead, not something imagined or hoping beyond reason they would see their loved one again one day when they walked through the front door. No sense of wondering *what if* or *what may*. Too bad she was wrong on all accounts. She was otherwise one in thousands of students in my career but I remembered that one fine detail about her and it has its place now.

I remembered the open casket in the funeral home. Mahogany-paneled walls with glass and brass sconces, burning a sickly yellow light reflecting off the high-white ceiling. I suppose it was an imitation of candlelight to add solemnity and comfort to the occasion. Personally, it made me feel almost as sick as seeing her lying there in the coffin, touched up by makeup and chemicals to look as I remembered her. The worry line in her forehead was gone, as were the crow's feet at the corners of her eyes, her cheeks rouged and lips glossed. Her eyes were closed as if in peaceful sleep, but I know her last night's sleep was anything but peaceful. Her Sunflower perfume wafted up from the open lid, filling the room with her scent, and she was nothing like I remembered her. It frightens me to no end.

I imagined her in her younger days and how little she did wear makeup. She would not have approved of this, and yet again I let her down by allowing even this, as in all things relating to her death. Not just the makeup, but the coffin, the crowd of bystanders. Only the Sunflower perfume was truly a part of her and I hope it gives her some comfort.

Since we were old enough to truly contemplate death, we've had the arrangement that she would be cremated with a small celebration of her life. No big shows, no major efforts to save her, just her surrounded by friends and family around her ashes. I was the one who wanted all the pomp and circumstances. She was dead now because of me and I was too selfish to even allow for her final wishes. Ashes to ashes, dust to dust, my will to see her again is a must! I can sense her disapproval, her accusations, and I shudder from them. So many years of happiness and trust now cast aside from her final moments until now. All because of me. What have I become?

Natural causes were the official results of the autopsy, but I knew different. Oh, how I knew different with the tears of guilt and remorse rolling down my cheeks mistaken for tears of sadness and loss by my family and friends gathered around me.

My sons reached out awkwardly, clasping my shoulders, while my daughter hugged me close, her own tears wetting the front of my black suit. It wasn't that I wasn't sad or heartbroken by my loss; indeed I felt that more than anything. Yet guilt and remorse are heavy emotions to bear and just as crippling to an old man such as myself. In the spectrum of emotions, guilt and remorse indeed weigh the heaviest.

How do I carry on with this guilt? Why did I not have the strength to end my own life that night after taking hers, sparing me all of this pain? Perhaps I did not deserve rest or peace after what I had done. Perhaps this and more is what I deserve.

Her eyes open and she looks me, and those thoughts are echoed there. I want to stare into her eyes forever. She is my beloved, but she closes her eyes as the pastor walks up to me and touches my arm. "It's time," he says.

The eulogy and remembrance ceremony were heartfelt and emotional, with much tearing and the occasional chuckle and fond smile. Her brother spoke of her youth as a surfer many decades before, and her youthful challenge to nature by going out into the incoming hurricane surf.

Her nephew spoke of how she was his second mother, and my own children from a previous marriage speak of her as if she was their true mother. Even our live-in nurse rose to speak of her in caring and fondness. Friends and colleagues went on about her many accomplishments in life, and through it all memories of our forty-five wonderful years relived themselves in my mind. They are wonderful memories, one after another, each interrupted by those final moments of her life, by my own shame over what I have done.

I welcomed the interruptions, not deserving even a moment of peace or happiness, contemplating our lives together, for in the end none of it matters after what I have done.

When it was my time to speak, my children, our friends, our live-in nurse, colleagues and church members, all watched me expectantly as I rose and walked to the podium next to her casket. I am too choked up to talk, something that my own friends and family feels uncomfortable with. For thirty years I made my living speaking in front of dozens and even hundreds of students at a time. Lecturing more than speaking perhaps, but with so many opinions and so little time on this earth, I was never without words, especially when it came to my own well of knowledge regarding history.

All of past experience was for naught though as I stood beside her, recoiling from my sins and deeds, as the sickish yellow light casting shadows upon her features. Her makeup which was never part of her, except on those rare occasions, reflected the pallid yellow light of the sconces, scarring her face and adding to the morbidity of the situation. Her eyes open again to stare at me, and in my head I hear her yelling, screaming at what I did to her that night, what I was doing to her now. *Oh, what have I done?* My voice echoes inside my head, screaming out in pain and frustration until I feel the lights burst inside me, welcoming the pain and darkness.

I'm told I was out for the better part of two days, though I recall nothing of that period. I awoke in the hospital with our live-in nurse beside me, telling me how I had suffered a stroke. I was allowed to go home so my sons can take care of me, making sure I am fed and clothed and that my dogs are taken care of.

The nurse is there as well, delegating duties, errands and chores with the efficiency of a drill sergeant readying their troops. At first I was fearful that I spoke aloud my horrendous deed, and they looked at me with accusatory glances so often that I knew I must have. *Did I tell them?* I wondered. Did I tell them how I killed their second mother, my beloved? My oldest child will hardly speak to me, nearly tossing my plates of food at me, much as you would a bone to a dog. My youngest son speaks a lot, nothing of importance, nothing of what I have done, and nothing of her. It is forced, like he would speak to someone he despises but is forced in civil society to discuss the weather with. I try to find the words to explain why, but the words fail me, as does my left side. I don't have words. Not because I can't talk but because I don't understand myself why I did what I did to my beloved of forty-five years.

Alas, either I did not speak or they kept my secret, as the police never showed up to handcuff me and take me away as I knew in my heart they should. Would confessing and turning myself in rectify anything? Would my guilt leave me as the passing of a summertime breeze, leaving me refreshed and feeling anew?

My nurse reminded me of my deed and told me my secret was safe. Safe with her. Safe with my beloved. I don't believe her when she says it's safe from me. Only if the stroke had killed me, put me out of my misery. As soon as these thoughts come though, so do others, a life full of memories with my beloved, and now her staring at me with those dead and lifeless eyes, wanting me to feel every inch of pain that I feel and more.

I would gladly take that pain and beg for more if it would mean she would forgive me. It is only her that can forgive me now, for surely I can not forgive myself.

It has been two weeks since the funeral and the obligatory casseroles and soups leftover from well wishers of an old widower were all but gone. My sons and daughter went back to their own families and I am left alone in our…*my* house. The nurse is there of course, but years of servitude has allowed her to blend into the home, invisible and quiet as a ghost, except the clicking of her heels as she walks the original wooden floors in the hallways. Pulling the covers up and over myself, I snuggle into the sheets, waiting to feel resistance as I press against my wife who is no longer there, but whose presence is still very much alive. I hear her calling out to me, asking me why. I fell into a restless sleep and dreamed of our last night together, smelling her perfume that must still be embedded into the pillows.

The dogs always keep me company, though for the most part they just settle down on the back porch, waiting for nightfall to come clamoring in on the couch and chairs, except the smallest one, the Dotson who takes up residency under our bed. I have bad dreams and my wife visits me, reminding me over and over how I betrayed her. The Dotson soon leaves my bedroom and sleeps under an end table in the living room. He's not alone, as soon the other dogs will only greet me with growls and snarls, the man who betrayed his beloved, their food lady, their human mother.

Waking one morning, I feel groggy and swear I can sense her next to me. As I roll over to swing my arm and leg over her, I shout in alarm when I feel her comforting presence there. No, not comforting, but angry, accusing, and I stare into her dead, lifeless eyes and smelling Sunflowers.

Screaming, I jump out of bed as fast as I used to be able to in my youth, but she's gone. I shudder and cry, falling to my knees and begging for her to forgive me.

There is no answer and I shuffle off to the shower, the dogs whimpering with their tails between their legs as I let them outside on my way to wash away my sins. Afterwards, while shaving, I swear I can still sense her, even see her out of the corner of my eye but when I turn with my heart in my throat, she isn't there. The smell of Sunflowers is thick in the air, as if exhaled from the lungs of a smoker. The nurse's heels click along the hallway as if nothing had happened.

The days pass, and eventually so do weeks, and I guess it's about the third month after the funeral when my daughter came by to check on me. I've never been one to clean up after myself and she became horrified at the conditions of the place, with laundry, dishes and assorted messes all over the house. She told me I look like a ghost and I explain to her how that is exactly what I am, a ghost. Lost and forgotten, paying for my sins and for…my beloved. She yelled at my nurse for not taking better care of me or my home, then threatened to fire her.

I stood up to her and for my nurse. It's my home after all. She shook her head at me and tried to comfort me, but I yelped as in the middle of the embrace, I saw my beloved standing behind her, watching us like she used to.

No, not like she used to. She would watch us fondly with a smile of joy and pride that equaled the love of the embrace. Today though, it was stern, angry and accusing, and reaching out to tear us apart.

What right did I have to be comforted by a loved one after what I did to her? What right did I have to be loved or to love after what I had done?

I pushed my daughter away and kicked her out of my house. She stood pleading with me as I locked the doors and shuffled around the house, ensuring that all of the other doors and windows were locked. My wife looked on, nodding in approval. I begged her to forgive me, wished for everything to be taken back, but she turned her back on me and faded away down the hallway, leaving me more alone than I could ever remember. I wanted to die but also I wanted to live, to wallow in this self-pity, loathing and guilt. After all, isn't this what I deserve after what I did to her?

Both of my sons came by later that evening but I sat up on the bed in the darkness and wished for quiet, telling my nurse to send them away. I wanted quiet from my sons beating on the front door and rattling the back sliding glass door as well. I wanted quiet from the baying of my dogs still left outside…did I hear all three of them or only two? Now that I think about it, I don't remember seeing the Dotson for a couple of days. I wonder if he found a new couple, a couple who wouldn't be torn apart by my treachery and betrayal. I wanted quiet from the creaks and groans of the house, one that was older than me. But not from the quiet of my wife as she reminded me of all the good years we had together and the horrible moment when I killed her. What she reminded me is what I should remember. Not those happy times, for what right did I have to them after what I'd done?

A few days later they came to take me away to an assisted living facility. I resisted as much as I could, screaming how they couldn't take me away from my beloved, wishing she would forgive me and come tell them that she would take care of me like always and to leave me be. To have her take me back inside, hold me, comfort me and take care of me as she did for all those years.

Yet in repayment for what I did to her, there is only silence. I don't deserve her, not even our memories, especially the happy ones, and perhaps only the last ones of her dying and her lying in the coffin that she never wanted

Alas, youth has strength that these old bones simply don't have anymore and I found myself in a cold dark room, the floor and ceiling covered in tile, the walls a bright white that even with the lights out shined with an energy all their own.

I'm strapped down on a cold vinyl mattress so I can't hurt myself, they say, but I know it is so I can't escape. They don't understand. I don't seek to escape but to return to the scene of my crime and wallow there until it is my time to go. They don't care. They don't listen.

Not like she had done for all of those years. The tears roll down my face for the millionth time and I plead with a God I don't believe in to have my wife back, to take back how I killed her. I smell her perfume but I'm not comforted. Her spirit softly replies that she is glad it doesn't.

Someone must have heard all the pleading, as the next few days I was escorted to a grief counselor who showed me the autopsy, went through the official reports of her death, and reminded me that it wasn't my fault. I can't take it anymore and I confess how it was I who, when I woke up when she was having her heart attack, turned my back to her and went back to sleep.

I confess that she was counting on me to rescue her, to save her, and all I did was roll over, ignoring her. The doctor tried to comfort me, but I am inconsolable and was given a sedative and taken to my room.

I am told my live-in nurse came and told the doctor how she had found my wife, how she supposedly had found me. Since I am not taken away or told otherwise, I assume she lies. Why? Why would she do such a thing? Surely she witnessed how I killed her, how I left her. How could she protect me!

Tonight my wife came to me again. I know it's her from the smell of her perfume, settling around me like a blanket in the wintertime.

How she found me here I have no idea, but she is accusing and tells me it is my time to die now, and for her to do nothing but watch. I plead with her, begging for forgiveness, reminding her how it was her wish to die without interference. I want to live with my guilt and remorse forever.

She reminds me as I fade away, dying with no one to witness, no one to hold me and no one to care, she reminds me of how this had always been my greatest fear.

It's what I deserve though, and for one instant I remember what it's like to feel at peace for a moment, knowing I am finally getting what I deserve and will go to Hell.

The last thing I hear is the click of heels walking away.

MIDNIGHT SNACKS

JOHN SKERCHOCK

Zach ran through the woods, hoping to out-distance the dead thing that was chasing him. He came upon it while trying to get home. It was there, in the clearing, standing still and staring at its feet, and he almost ran smack into it. That's when it saw Zach and began to move. Slowly at first, but as its decaying joints became more animated, movement was quick though clumsy. And it was coming after young Zachary Martin.

Zach left the farmhouse later than he should have. It was tough to sneak out with Momma watching. Now it was getting dark. He had to be careful because the dead things were more active in the dark. But Zach had become distracted. It was his first time out alone since the 'Crisis' began. He'd gone too far from home trying to do his part searching for food and supplies. He'd checked the Haney farm, but the old, white-sided house was burned to the ground, and the barn was empty. He knew he was causing worry back home. Momma would tan his hide the minute he walked through the gate so he wanted the beating to be worth it. He wanted to come home with enough to fill their bellies.

The dead thing was old Parson Sedgwick. The parson was one of the first people to go when the Crisis came. He was pretty well spent, almost rotted away. Bits of flesh still clung to his bones, but most of the meat had fallen off. The eyeballs—without eyelids or flesh around the cheeks—looked grotesquely large, like bulging, white egg shells with tiny black dots for pupils. They looked like they would roll out of his head at any moment.

By Zach's experience, the parson should have crumpled into a heap a long time ago. Maybe faith kept him together? Maybe God or the Devil wouldn't let him rest? He shambled purposefully in Zach's direction.

The first time Zach had seen a dead thing, he and Pa were in town. They'd heard about the weird doings on the radio. Pa had Zach's older brothers Billy and Toby started protecting the farm while they took the old Chevy pick-up into town to see if they could help.

They found the town deserted, and a few cars were parked on the street. Some doors to homes were wide open, and others were busted open like someone had tried to get in them. Pa wondered aloud if scavengers or rescuers had caused the damage.

The smell of smoke filled the air. It smelled like barbecued chicken and Zach's mouth watered. Pa drove the truck as they followed the smell. Maybe the people on the radio were wrong? Maybe the Crisis was already over.

Around the corner, four blocks into town, they saw it. It was no chicken barbecue, it was a cremation pile. Bodies were stacked in heaps in the center of the intersection. They were charred and mutilated. When the breeze picked up, flames rose from the hot coals deep inside the pile of smoldering flesh.

Pa was always a strong man. He was like an oak tree, full of strength and energy. He opened the door of the truck and vomited on the street. Zach tasted salt on his lips and realized he was crying. Was this the end of the world?

That's when he saw his first dead thing. It was Mr. Bartal, the high school gym teacher. He'd been after Zach to join the track team. He was a short, stocky man with muscular arms and a huge, barrel-like chest. He had thick, black hair that he always kept neatly parted on the left. Only what Zach saw wasn't Mr. Bartal anymore. His chest was half-eaten, and his neat black hair was standing up in a punk-spiked style, with dried blood for support. He or it was staggering in their direction.

Zach let out a whimper, but Pa was ready. He'd heard the radio reports. He knew what to do. He reached into the bed of the truck and removed one of the sledgehammers that the boys had been using to sink fence posts into the ground along the southern field. The tool was heavy, but Pa lifted it without effort. He swung it fast and brought it down hard on Mr. Bartal's head. Zach heard a sound like throwing a big rock into thick mud, and the gym teacher collapsed into a heap.

Zach and his father left town in a hurry. They couldn't help anyone, and they didn't stop to help themselves by stocking up with fuel or food. Now they were starving.

Zach knew no matter how much of a head start he had, Parson Sedgwick would keep following him because he had caught Zach's *scent*, as his father called it. Once the dead things caught wind of you, they would follow until you were caught, or you had somehow managed to elude or destroy the things. Zach and his family had been holed up at the farm for a long time. They'd been able to elude the dead things…until now.

A few days after returning from town, the dead things seemed to be everywhere. It wasn't unusual to see them shamble through the fields, even in the day time. Zach and his brothers used to watch them through holes in the fence. They were scary at first, but like anything else, the boys got used to seeing them. The creatures started to look comical rather than frightening.

As time passed, they didn't see the things at all. Pa said he hadn't seen them in packs for a long time. He took the truck to look for supplies on Tuesday. Zach's oldest brother, Toby, rode shotgun. It was the last ride before the gas ran out. They came back empty handed. Pa said they didn't see nobody or no *thing*.

Maybe the dead are being put down by living survivors better equipped than the Martins or simply rotting away? Or maybe they'd found better feeding grounds. Zach shivered at that thought and kept running.

Pa always said ole Parson Sedgwick was a stubborn cuss. When the parson was alive, Pa used to comment how he should have met the Lord twenty years ago. Parson Sedgwick refused to be put down.

According to the radio, Zach knew survivors were fighting back. Groups of people were making an effort to get rid of the dead things. None of the raids had gotten Parson Sedgwick yet. He'd avoided the town during the burning. He was a wily one.

Darkness came. The evening gloomy that gave Zach what little light he had to navigate by was gone. The moon wasn't out yet and Zach couldn't safely find his way. He could only go so fast through the bushes and between the trees and he didn't want to stumble into another one of those things. A thing with a little more 'life' to it might be a lot quicker than the parson, and it would be the end of Zach for certain.

Zach was down to a slow trot. The path was getting narrower, the bushes bigger, and the sky even darker. He was still a ways from home, and now well into the forest, but it was too dark to judge just how far. He could holler for help, but it would probably do more harm than good. No one could help him out here.

Darkness was a bad sign. The dead things liked the night. Sunshine and bright lights held them at bay. Maybe that's why it had been so easy to get rid of most of them during the burnings. Still, a few managed to get away like the parson and claim more victims. They'd shamble about into towns, the woods, or in fields, where they'd find more victims or just rot away.

A grim realization hit Zach harder than a fist in the face. The path wasn't right. The stars were out and the sky was wrong. Zach was in unfamiliar territory. He was lost! As a child, he had roamed the woods around his house often. He knew every path, knew which fork to take, and what was and wasn't a short cut.

Now, in his desperation to get away from the parson, he had wandered too far off course. Zach started to shake. He didn't know if he could get home before the parson got him.

The darkness was oppressive. Zach stopped to get his bearings. Behind him, crashing through the bushes, the parson shambled onward. Zach began to worry that the parson's movement might attract other dead things his way. He had to do something and fast! Standing still was the wrong thing to do. A deer standing still is an easy target for a hunter. Zach felt like a deer—a scared, confused fawn looking for its mother.

With his heart almost in his throat, Zach ran into the darkness. He tripped over a rock and fell hard, banging his knee. His pants ripped as he went down. A shock of pain shot up his right side like a cold spike being driven through him with a hammer. He hurt and wasn't too sure he could move. Then he heard the sounds.

There were other things in the darkness! Dead things waiting for a sign now had a direction in which to go and Zach's noisy fall had given them the direction. They started to move. They seemed to be everywhere, but maybe he was overreacting?

His lungs constricting in fear, Zach struggled to breathe as he got back on his feet and tried to run. The pain in his right knee was excruciating. He could only hobble a few steps at a time. He bit his tongue to keep from screaming. He had to do better if he wanted to get away. Zach had no intention of being a midnight snack for some undead ghoul.

He looked around quickly, then took off running. He ran into a tree. It was there in front of him, but fear and the darkness had made it impossible for him to see. Zach went down with a thud. He saw stars in front of his face, then nothing.

When Zach came to, his head thumped with pain and he felt something dried and crusty under his nose. He tried rubbing it away. The pain in his knee had considerably lessened, but the throbbing in his head was unbearable!

Climbing slowly to his feet, Zach looked around. His eyes had adjusted somewhat to the darkness and he could make out shapes. Nothing moved, but he could hear a shallow grunting that he knew was the sound of a dead thing; the stench that assaulted his nose was overwhelming. It was a sticky sweet smell that clung to his nostrils. His stomach churned, but he fought back the bile that was slowly crawling up his throat. Some *thing* was very close to him.

As Zach's eyes focused, he could see one shape that was not as still as a tree. It was swaying from side to side as it moved forward. It was the parson, shambling blindly but purposefully towards him.

The moon began to rise over Bear Mountain. It cast pale rays down upon the dead thing. Zach could see its mouth chomping slowly. The lips and most of the cheeks had rotted away, leaving a big, toothy hole in place of its mouth. The creature's stench was in the still, warm air and it was noxious. Tears rolled down Zach's face.

Zach backed away very slowly, his feet carefully feeling everything they moved over or stepped on. He was preparing to turn and run when his right leg felt nothing underneath it. He stopped, turned his head, and looked down. He was at the edge of the quarry just at the end of Barry Dingmans' farm.

His heart dropped. He had nowhere to run and the dead thing was right there.

Tears filled Zach's eyes. He was terrified. He knew the thing would be on him in a second. It would tear the flesh from his body and devour it as Zach watched, dying. Then Zach would be a dead thing. He'd wander the woods, maybe even get home, and maybe even harm his family.

Zach began to shake uncontrollably. That's when Parson Sedgwick made a move. The thing lunged at him. All Zach could think to do was to drop to the ground. The dead thing hurdled over him and into the pit.

Zach breathed a sigh of relief as he heard the parson crash onto the stones below. Then he started to slide over the edge. Panic caused him to grab at the ground, fingers scraping deep into the dirt to slow his fall. It worked. He held onto the ground at the edge of the pit, but he knew in seconds he'd fall to his death. His feet couldn't find any purchase, and his hands had nothing solid to grasp. He was grabbing helplessly at dirt, roots, and weeds.

As Zach's grip on the edge was about to give way, an arm reached down and grabbed him. It clutched tightly to his left arm. Zach's savior had a lot of strength, and the handgrip was solid.

Zach looked up and saw the camouflaged sleeve. It was the military! They were here! Momma had always told him that if he couldn't find his way home then head for one of the military posts. The army had been seen in the valley. They were cleaning out the dead things. Zach couldn't wait to tell them about the survivors in the compound. They'd all be free again!

A feeling of warmth came over Zach as he was rescued. He didn't know what to say. He was so excited. He sniffled loudly and tried to laugh. As the hand brought him up from the edge of the pit, Zach saw the outline of a huge soldier, as the man lifted him straight out of the frying pan.

But as Zach rose higher, he could tell something was wrong. The soldier wasn't moving right. He wasn't saying anything either. He was clutching Zach tightly. Too tightly! Zach was lifted into the air until they were face to face.

Zach's hope was crushed. His eyes filled with terror as he got a closer look at his savior. The left side of the soldier's face was eaten away. Its tongue was dangling out of its cheek and licking the bottom of a dislodged eyeball. The soldier was a dead thing, and a relatively fresh dead thing, unlike the parson!

Zach screamed and kicked out, terrified. He hit the dead thing square in the chest, the soldier lost its grip, and Zach fell to the ground. He landed on his feet away from the edge of the pit. Zach thought about pushing the soldier into the pit, but the urge for flight was more immediate.

Zach took off in the same direction he had come. He didn't wait to see if the dead thing was following him. He knew it was. It was stronger than the parson and it would be faster. Zach knew he'd have to run fast if he wanted to save his hide, but he couldn't run fast because of the injury to his knee.

After what seemed like hours but was only a few minutes, Zach stumbled onto a path. He followed it downhill for an awfully long time. Suddenly, he knew where he was! He recognized the path as the old hunting trail he and his brothers used to use before the world went all screwy, and it would lead him to safety if he was lucky.

A short time later, when he passed Hunter's Rock, Zach knew he was almost home. A good thing, too, because he was very tired, his knee was screaming with pain, and his head felt like it was ready to split.

The dead soldier was still behind him.

Zach dashed down the hill and left the woods. He entered the field to the east of the farmhouse and the compound they had built to protect it. From across the field, Zach could see lights. It seemed so far away! Would anyone be out looking for him? Were there any dead things up ahead blocking his path? Zach didn't know. He only knew that he had to keep going or he would be dead.

He shouted as he got closer. "Momma! Pa! Open the gate! I'm coming home!" He shouted until his voice went hoarse. He didn't care if other dead things heard him now, not as long as he made it to the compound.

Zach didn't know if anyone heard him. His lungs screamed with pain. His knee wanted to explode. He had to stop and catch his breath, rub his knee. As he did, he chanced a look behind him. The dead thing had fallen and rolled to the bottom of the hill. It got up quickly, at least at a pace faster than Zach had known a dead thing could move, and it took off after him. It wasn't very close to him at first, but it was gaining!

Zach started to run again. His legs were cramping up. His knee was about to give out. The dead thing was too fast. It was closing the gap between them and Zach didn't know if he could make it.

Within twenty feet of the compound, Zach started yelling again. The gate opened and Billy and Toby began calling to him. Looking over his shoulder, Zach could see the soldier only a few feet behind him. Dead things didn't feel pain, he thought, and from the way this one moved it hadn't been dead long at all.

"You're almost here, boy!" shouted Pa.

Sanctuary was in sight! Ignoring the pain, Zach ran through the gate with his brothers cheering him on.

"The gate!" Toby cried.

The dead thing ran into the compound before Pa could close the gate. Billy and Toby jumped behind the dead soldier, prodding and hitting it with two by fours. They were pushing it towards the fire. Over the flames was a large black kettle they'd used for making apple butter during happier times. Now it held more than twenty gallons of boiling water.

Pa slammed the bolt home, locking the gate. No other dead things would be getting in tonight!

Meanwhile, the boys were spinning the soldier around and around as they whacked and poked it. It couldn't gain footing. It was hopelessly unbalanced. Then gravity took over and the soldier fell into the pot.

At the sound of the splash everyone cheered. Billy kept whacking the dead thing until its head split open and gray brain matter oozed into the soup. The soldier jerked violently for an instant, then sank under the water with a gurgle.

After the thing was in the boiling water for a few minutes, Momma began to stir it with a large wooden spoon. She added a handful of garlic cloves and a bushel of potatoes. Soon the meat turned white and broke away from the bone.

The boys watched as Momma cooked. Hunger pangs would soon become a thing of the past. Zach looked at the kettle with anticipation.

Already the aches and pains were starting to subside as he realized his adventure had been worth the effort. It would be around midnight when they would finally get to eat.

Zach hoped the meal would be worth the wait, and he prayed that it would be a while before they asked him again to be the bait.

CLACK

TERRY ALEXANDER

*T*hose shoes, those damn wooden-soled shoes. Lenny Fletcher clamped his hands over his ears. *Doesn't that bitch have any other shoes?* His teeth sank into his bottom lip; the coppery taste of blood filled his mouth.

He crossed the small cell and stared through the wire-reinforced door glass. Ruth Pascoe plodded down the hallway, packing an armload of patient files. She blew an unruly strand of dark hair from her face. Her brown open-toed shoes double-clacked on the tile floor. *Clack clack, clack clack.* Heel toe, heel toe.

Dr. Pascoe shifted her bundle and glanced at her watch. "Damn it, I'm late." She quickened her pace, and the horrendous sound of the clacking shoes grew louder. "Mr. Fletcher, we have a session in one hour," She glanced at Lenny's face as she hurried on toward her office.

Lenny's downcast eyes settled on the floor. He caught a glimpse of red toenails as the doctor walked by his door. A barrage of nightmare-images assaulted his consciousness. He squeezed his eyes together.

Thick drops were splattered on white walls.

"Please, not today!" he shouted after her. "I'm sick, I'm not feeling good."

"One hour, Mr. Fletcher." She disappeared from sight and the echo of her footsteps slowly faded.

He rushed to his bunk and threw himself into the embrace of the flame-resistant mattress. The entire cell was constructed for the safety of the patients to prevent self-injury. The sheets, blankets, and even the pillow, were all fire-proof. Light fixtures were recessed and the wiring was unreachable without a special tool.

Lenny was here to pay a price—the state didn't want to be cheated out of its pound of flesh.

"Those damn shoes," he mumbled. "Those damn shoes. I hate those fucking shoes." Lenny rocked back and forth. "I can't stand the noise. I can't stand it!"

A familiar voice spoke within the room, "Well, do something about it. Don't just whine…do something."

Lenny stopped and glanced around the cell, looking for the speaker. His jaw quivered. "Who's there? Who said that?" Lenny cocked his head to the side and frantically searched the shadowed corners of his tiny cell. He knew that he was alone, but he'd heard that voice before…

A hard rap echoed upon his metal door and another, more lamentable voice commanded him from outside the cell. "Come on, Fletcher. Get your sorry ass over here. It's time to go see the head-shrinker."

A shiver ran along Lenny's spine. He recognized Ralph Sweeney's harsh voice. Sweeney enjoyed his reputation as the cruelest officer on staff. He delighted in the mistreatment of the Rumbolt patients. Lenny had suffered at his hands many times.

Once again, the oddly recognizable, male voice spoke within Lenny's cell. "Don't let that fucker push you around, do something bad to his ass. Then he'll leave you alone."

Sweeny rattled the chains and pounded on the door. "Damn it! Hurry up, you piece of shit. I've got other things to do."

"Go…" Lenny stilled his tongue. "Tell her I don't feel well today. Ask her if we can have our session t…t…tomorrow," Lenny stuttered.

"Get your ass over here, now!" Sweeney's voice hardened. "Don't make me call the goons."

Everyone at Rumbolt knew about the goons—they were Sweeney's hand-picked followers. They were cruel, sadistic men, each one more than willing to administer a beating or inflict some form of torture at Sweeny's whim. None of the patients dared to raise Captain Sweeny's ire.

"Give me a minute." Lenny ran his fingers through his hair; combs and mirrors weren't allowed in this wing of the facility.

"Hurry up, we don't have all day."

Lenny crossed the cell slowly, staring at the closed bean-hole at the bottom of the door. He bit his lower lip. Dread gnawed at the pit of his stomach. His eyes closed at the sound of jingling keys, waiting for the metal-on-metal shriek as the large brass key slid into the lock. A tremor ran through his body as the lower lock clacked open.

"Come on, you know the drill, stick your feet through," Sweeney ordered.

Lenny dropped to his butt and twisted his feet through the opening. The cold kiss of the leg irons embraced his ankles. He moved his feet inside and repeated the procedure with his hands. Sweeney squeezed the handcuffs tight around his wrists.

"All right, maggot, on your feet." Sweeney slammed the lower door closed, then fitted the key into the lock on the main door.

Lenny's teeth sank into his mangled lower lip, waiting for the inevitable clack. The loud noise grated on his nerves like sandpaper peeling away layers of wood. The door squealed as it swung open.

Sweeney's hand closed on his shoulder. "Come on, damn it." His fingers squeezed the tendon leading to Lenny's neck.

Lenny gritted his teeth. He ignored the pain, unwilling to give Sweeney the pleasure of seeing him wince. The leg irons jingled as he shuffled down the corridor to Dr. Pascoe's office.

"Thank you, Mr. Sweeney," her bright smile dazzled the officer. "Mr. Fletcher, take a seat, please."

Lenny kept his eyes focused on the floor. He knew the exact number of steps to the uncomfortable chair, having made the trip more times than he cared to remember. He settled into its lumpy cushion, as Dr. Pascoe walked to her large chair behind the ornate desk. Her wooden soles clacked on the floor and sent shivers tingling up his spine.

"Look at me, Mr. Fletcher," she said sternly.

He unwillingly met her eyes. Frown lines marred her smooth forehead. "Yes, Dr. Pascoe," Lenny said.

"How are you…today?" She placed heavy emphasis on the last word. "Are the voices still a problem?"

"No," his jaw quivered. "They're not a problem."

"Mr. Fletcher, I've been at Rumbolt for over a year. During that time, I've worked very closely with you, but I don't think we've made any progress." She brushed a lock of hair from her eyes.

His fingers began to twitch. "I'm fine. Really, I'm fine. Just let me go back to my cell."

"You were married before you came here. Isn't that correct?" she asked. "Wasn't her name Marie?"

The twitching increased. "Dr. Pascoe, please let me go back to my cell," Lenny pleaded.

"Didn't you kill your wife? Didn't you shoot her when you found her with another man?"

"No, no, that's not what happened." He jumped to his feet. "Please, let me go back to my cell!"

His fragmented mind was bombarded with macabre imagery. *Thick crimson drops splattered against a bone-white wall and dripped slowly upon a hardwood floor. Bright red fingernails, hard to distinguish from all the blood pooling on the floor. A woman's face, beautiful and laughing one instant, then dead the next, a black hole between her still-open eyes as scarlet blood oozed out of the hole and slid between the fissures and valleys of her face.*

"You killed Marie in a fit of rage, didn't you?"

"No!" Lenny balled his fists and shouted. "Damn it, I didn't kill my wife. I didn't kill her."

Empty bullet casings flew from the ejection port of the .380, which clattered to the floor. Clack, clack, clack, clack. Funny he didn't hear the discharge of the pistol, but he heard the sound of the empty shells strike the floor.

"Mr. Fletcher, you need to sit down." Her mouth drew into a firm, straight line. "You need to sit down now."

"You bitch!" Spittle frothed upon Lenny's lips. "You know I didn't kill my wife. You know I didn't kill Marie!"

A lifeless hand draped over the edge of the mattress. Dark red fingertips brushed the floor, tracing a line in the circle of blood.

A scream erupted from Dr. Pascoe in the confined space. "Sweeney! Captain Sweeney, get in here!"

The officer bull-rushed through the door, which rebounded from the wall. "Fletcher, sit down now, you piece of shit." Sweeney tugged a Taser from his duty belt. "Damn it, I said sit down!"

"I didn't kill my wife," Lenny turned, screaming. "I'm telling you I didn't kill her!"

Scarlet fingernails, the same color as her blood.

"Sit down, Mr. Fletcher." Dr. Pascoe reached for his arm. He pulled away from her touch.

"I'll make you sit down." Sweeney lined the sight; his itchy finger squeezed the trigger.

The sharp barbs struck Lenny's chest and penetrated his bright orange jumpsuit. "No!" he screamed. The electrical shock buzzed through his body. His muscles stiffened. He fell to the floor, unable to control his writhing, convulsing body. His blinking eyes focused on Sweeney. The officer smiled broadly.

Sweeney shook his head. "Crazy bastard, I knew he was going to twist off today." The captain closed on the prone man.

"Mr. Sweeney, take him back to his cell." Dr. Pascoe's fists rested on her hips. "I was hoping that confrontation therapy would show some results. I underestimated his level of psychosis."

"You sorry bastard." Sweeney lashed out with his heavy black boots and kicked Lenny in the ribs with such force that the paralyzed, helpless patient was lifted from his knees.

"Please, no more," Lenny mumbled.

The boot landed again in the defenseless man's side. "I'm going to really give you something to think about."

Pascoe intervened. "Mr. Sweeney, that's enough. Take him back to his cell."

"Yeah, Doc, but this maggot needs to learn a lesson, and I'm just the fella to teach him." Sweeney lifted the walkie talkie to his lips. "Brisbane, this is Sweeney. Come to the psych department. I need a little help."

Lenny awoke hours later. He tried to move his arms and legs, but four-point restraints held him fast to the bed. He gazed out the single window.

Late afternoon sunlight gleamed brightly through the reinforced glass. Lenny's mind ran amok. *Oh, hell, what happened? What did I do now?*

"You really screwed the pooch this time."

He spun his head at the sound of the voice. It was the same voice that tormented him before Sweeney summoned him to another painful meeting with Dr. Pascoe.

A shadowy shape sat in the straight-backed chair by the metal desktop. The lower portion of an orange clad jumpsuit caught his eyes, the upper body was clad in darkness.

"Who are you? How did you get in here?" Lenny demanded.

"Sweeney and his goons will be paying you a visit shortly. They're really gonna fuck you up this time."

"I didn't mean to d...d...d...do anything," Lenny stammered. "It's wasn't my fault, I can't stand the n...n...noise." He shivered uncontrollably. Lenny had past experiences with the goons. They were a hardcore bunch and enjoyed inflicting pain and torture at the slightest provocation.

But he was also sure that he had a past experience with the shadowed stranger.

"Sweeney enjoys bustin' heads," the stranger reminded him. "I told you this would happen. I told you they were going to screw you over. You've got to take a stand, get your life back under control. Show these fuckers that you mean business, that you can take care of yourself."

"I'm trying to get out of here." Lenny strained against the bonds. "I just want to go home."

"You're not getting it. You're never going home. You'll be here till it's time for the old dirt nap." The speaker crossed his legs. "And if you're not careful, you'll be enjoying your nap soon. If you're going to survive, you need to get a sticker."

"I can't do that. I'm not a killer. I just want to go home to Marie," Lenny sobbed. "I just want to go home."

"You're a killer, buddy boy. You killed Marie. You emptied a clip in her and that bastard she was screwing." The shape leaned forward into the light.

It wore Lenny's face.

"Get a sticker," the stranger suggested. "Do what you know best."

"No! No, I didn't kill Marie. I loved her." Lenny shook his head and struggled against the restraints.

"Yeah, we loved her so much we popped that final cap right between her eyes. You remember how that red circle looked while it oozed blood down her nose?"

"Wake up, buttercup." Sweeney's burly frame filled the doorway. "You've got company." He walked into the cell with three of his goons trailing behind him.

"No, please leave me alone. I won't d…d…do anything wrong again. I'll follow the rules. I swear I won't d…d…do anything wrong again," Lenny begged.

"Oh, I know you won't, but me and the boys are going to give you some incentive." A wide smile wrinkled Sweeney's face.

The first blow split Lenny's cheek; warm blood poured down Lenny's throat, causing him to gag. He spat some of the blood out of his mouth and felt it thread down his chin until it cooled upon his neck. "No more. Please, no more. I've learned my lesson. I won't act up again."

"Damn right, you won't." Sweeney's toothy smile broadened.

"Come on, boys, that's enough. I think buttercup's learned his lesson." Sweeney stopped his goons after five minutes.

Lenny lay unconscious in blood-soaked sheets. A bloody froth bubbling from his lips gave the only indication he still drew breath. His swollen eyes opened to small slits. He tried to focus on the blurry figure in the chair. The shape seemed to bulge and curl in on itself.

"I told you this would happen." Lenny's own voice mocked him. "Next time, they'll kill you and tell everyone you attacked them. You've got to grow some gonads and protect yourself. "

"How? How can I do that?" Blood sprayed from his pulped lips.

The doppelganger smiled. "I hear the orderly coming. He'll take you to medical."

"Wait, don't leave now, help me. Help me!" Lenny screamed.

Riley Cooper peered through the doorway. "Lenny, it's supper time. Why's your door open? You know they have a fit when someone picks a lock around here." He ventured into the cell. His bulging eyes gaped at the blood-drenched figure bound to the bed.

"Damn, what happened? Did you piss Sweeney off?" Riley hurriedly loosened the straps. "Man, the goons really did a job on you. Come on, I'll get you to medical."

"No." Lenny shook his head. The movement sent fresh shards of pain through his body. "No medical."

"They beat the shit out of you. You need Doc to look at those cuts and bruises." Riley loosened the bonds at his ankles. "What did you do to get four-pointed?"

Lenny spit a mouthful of blood to the floor. "I yelled at Pascoe."

Riley shook his head. "Bad move. You know that bitch is wiggy. Look, you wanna try to eat something? It's not bad tonight."

"Just leave it on the table. Riley, please don't say anything about this. I don't want anymore trouble with the goons."

The orderly placed the tray on the table. "You really need to see the doctor. You can tell them you fell or something." Riley shook his head.

"Naw, I'll be okay." Lenny attempted a smile. "Just don't forget me for rec tomorrow. I missed it today."

"Are you kidding?" Riley stood in the doorway, his hands fidgeting with the keys. "You think they'll let you go outside or hang out in the rec room?"

"I want rec tomorrow." Lenny pressed his blood soaked pillowcase against his face.

"Yeah, whatever you say. I wouldn't want you to miss it."

"Riley, you're an all right guy for a staff member." Lenny stumbled to the desk.

Riley pulled the door closed and locked it. Lenny didn't register the clack.

"So, you're gonna take my advice. You're gonna get a sticker." The voice had moved to the blood-stained bed.

"Yeah, I'm gonna get a sticker." Lenny pulled the tray toward him. He sank a plastic spork into the mashed potatoes. "I've got to figure out who has one."

"Let me out. I know how to find one."

The late afternoon sun streamed through the window. The wire embedded in the thick glass cast a checkerboard pattern on Lenny's face. He lifted a hand to his pounding head and swung his legs to the floor. His eyes fastened on a fifteen-inch length of ten-gauge wire on the desktop.

"I told you…I know who keeps the good stuff."

A shadowy figure leaned against the door. "Where did you get it?" Lenny mumbled.

"Barney Reynolds. I told him I'd break his jaw and shit down his throat if he didn't come off it."

"The drooler. I didn't think he had enough going on upstairs to get a sticker." Lenny massaged his temples.

"Don't let Barney fool you. He's got more going on upstairs than anyone thinks. Tomorrow you'll see Dr. Pascoe again. Make it count."

"I will," Lenny nodded. "I will."

Lenny stood on tip-toes to peer through the glass. He heard Dr. Pascoe's footsteps long before he saw her hurrying down the corridor. *Clack clack, clack clack,* her hard-soled shoes echoed on the tile floor. Lenny cringed at every step. Each footfall sent fresh shivers of agony twisting inside his brain.

"Why?" he mumbled. "Why is she wearing those shoes again?" His fingers touched the stiff wire hidden in the sleeve of his jumpsuit. "Today's the day. Today's the day."

"Sweeney will be here in a few minutes," the doppelganger explained. "Stick him when he opens the bean-hole and get the keys. You can stretch your arm and get the key in the main lock, one simple twist and you're free."

"Yeah, I know." Lenny closed his eyes. He licked his lips nervously. A tremor ran the length of his body.

"I'll do it for you," the voice offered. "I'm a killer. I killed Marie and that bastard she was boning."

"So did I," Lenny nodded as an image erupted through his mind.

A young, nude woman reclined on a queen-sized bed, her face stretched in a satisfied smile. Her dark hair framed her face, lending it a natural glow. The vision abruptly changed. *Dark crimson stained the bed. The woman's bullet-riddled body was frozen in death. Scarlet dripped from a raw, bloody hole in her forehead.*

"Come on, maggot." Sweeney rapped on the cell door. "Time to see the doc." He bent down and unlocked the security port. The lock clacked loudly.

Lenny cringed. "Just a minute. I'm not ready." He knelt by the door.

"Hurry up," Sweeney quickly grew impatient. He rapped on the door again. "Come on, damn it."

Lenny bit his lip while his heart drummed loudly in his chest; he was certain that Sweeny could hear its incessant hammering.

The officer squatted. His face was framed by the rectangular opening. "What the hell is wrong with you, Fletcher? Maybe my boys should pay you another visit."

Lenny drove his arm forward. The stiff wire struck Sweeney's eyeball. The sharp point cracked through the orbital bone toward the officer's brain. Thick fluid gushed from the socket.

Sweeney fell to the floor and quivered. His right hand pawed weakly at the weapon. "Damn you, Fletcher, I'm gonna kill you!" He rolled across the floor as his hands fastened on the metal wire. He lacked the strength and willpower to yank it free.

Lenny reached through the security port. He bent his arm to blindly locate the key and tugged it from the bean-hole lock. He pressed his shoulder against the port while reaching up with the key in his hand, his fingers groping for the main lock. He located the device, and he struggled to fit the key inside.

"You're dead! Do you hear me, Fletcher? You're dead!" Sweeney tugged on the blood-slick wire.

Finally, the key grated inside the lock. Lenny's fingertips managed to grasp the brass ring. The stiff lock clacked and Lenny shoved the door open. He stretched his cramped muscles and stepped out into the corridor.

"You're going to kill me, huh? I don't think I'll give you the chance." Lenny glared at the brutal man, who writhed in agony on the tiles.

Sweeney desperately keyed his mic. "Officer down send help, C block," he mumbled.

"Repeat last transmission." Loud static echoed from the speaker.

"Officer down, C block," he repeated.

Lenny lashed out. He kicked Sweeney's ribs several times, lifting the injured man from the floor. "You're a piece of shit, Sweeney." His hand closed on the makeshift weapon, wrenching it free.

A loud slurping noise filled the hallway.

A thin smile crossed Lenny's face. He knelt beside Sweeney and drove the heavy-gauge wire into his tormentor's throat. "Save me a place in hell."

Sweeney gurgled. A bloody air bubble burst upon his lips. His remaining eye narrowed to blue flint. A final shudder quaked through his body.

Lenny yanked his weapon free and marched toward Pascoe's office. There wasn't much time—the goons were on their way. He passed through the open doorway leading to the psychologist's office. He stood before Dr. Pascoe's window, his face centered in the square, waiting for her to see him. A minute went by. Sweat trickled down Lenny's face.

His mind raced: *Hurry up. The goons will be here soon!*

Lenny licked his lips. He resisted the temptation to knock.

Pascoe's amber eyes lifted from her paperwork. She smiled broadly as she rose from her desk chair. Her shoes clacked loudly across the pastel floor tile. "Come in, Sweeney. Bring him in, please." She pulled the door open.

Lenny's right arm darted forward, and buried the heavy wire in the doctor's shoulder; a geyser of blood sprayed Lenny's face. "Hello, Dr. Pascoe." Lenny pushed her to the floor. With a fistful of her hair in his hand, he dragged her to the large desk, leaving a thin trail of blood. Lenny rummaging through her purse found the keys and locked the office door.

"You can't get away with this. Fletcher, they'll kill you." Tears streamed down her face. Blood leaked between her fingers, dripping to the floor. Lenny shoved her fancy desk in front of the door—the metal legs scraped across the tiles as he constructed his makeshift barricade.

"I know, Doctor, but before they kill me, I'll make you regret you were ever born." An evil grin lit his face. "We've got at least a half hour. A lot can happen in thirty minutes."

VENGEANCE COMES IN ALL SIZES

ANTHONY GIANGREGORIO

The revolver with the matte finish was so close to Sharon's face she could smell the gun oil. She closed her eyes, tears sliding down her cheeks, as she battled her own body not to piss herself in terror.

"If you even think of leaving me, I swear to fucking God I'll kill you. And if you actually try, I'll kill the children."

Her husband's voice was hoarse, from smoking his entire life. Sharon winced when he spit into her face, each bit of saliva that hit her skin like a hard slap.

"Are you fucking listening to me, you bitch! You fucking whore!" He took the gun from her face but he still stood before her. "I don't know why I married a cow like you. Look at you, you're fat and you look like shit. Would it fucking kill you to take a shower and wash and comb your hair once in a while?" He seemed to pause, or so she thought. "Maybe that's why I have to fuck hookers, 'cause you sure as shit can't give me what I want anymore."

The tears were flowing harder now, but her mouth was closed tight, and she fought back the urge to break down and really cry. Sharon knew if she started, she wouldn't be able to stop and Charlie didn't like it when she cried.

"Fuck," he hissed. "You're pathetic."

She heard him turn and walk away. Cracking one eye, then the other, she found herself alone in their bedroom. A few seconds later the front door slammed, the car engine started, and Charlie was driving away, on his way to work.

But he would be back.

He always came back.

She found she couldn't stand anymore, and her legs, which were already weak, now collapsed beneath her. She slumped to the floor, her forehead touching the carpet, sobbing hard, her arms wrapped around her as she slowly rocked her body.

How did her life get like this? How did she become the slave to a man who said he once loved her? She cried for a full ten minutes and then gathered herself, knowing if she looked like she was crying when Charlie returned home he would be angry. Her gaze went to underneath the bed and the small shoebox hidden in the far corner, near the wall. Inside that shoebox was a thousand dollars; money siphoned off from the grocery money Charlie gave her each week.

Though he checked the receipt each week, she had been able to keep a few dollars each shopping trip, sometimes even less than a dollar. Inside that shoebox was three year's worth of saving, scrimping and finding loose change in the street when she was allowed out with him. When she saw a penny or a dime, she would pretend she was tying her sneaker, and as Charlie waited impatiently, she would snatch it up. He was her slave master and she was never allowed out of his sight when they went out.

She sometimes would see a policeman and she wanted to run to the officer and beg for help but she couldn't. Because her children weren't safe. She was the only thing keeping them safe. If she ever ran from Charlie and didn't take them too…well, some things weren't worth dwelling on.

Besides, the police wouldn't help her, wouldn't believe her. They would take Charlie's side. And the reason was because he was one of them. Charlie had been a cop for over ten years, and if she ever tried to call the police for help, nothing would happen, even if they came to the house. Charlie would make it all go away when the police arrived at the house. He did before, back when she'd called the police once when he'd raised his hand to her a few years ago. She'd warned him if he ever did that, she would report him, but he had never seemed to care. Now she knew why.

She always tried to look at the bright side. Other than that one time, he'd never hit her, and in fact had never so much as slapped her or their two children since. Back then, she'd assumed it was because she had called the police when he had tried. But physical abuse wasn't the problem, it was the mental abuse. The threats, the jibes, the warnings, all of which she truly believed he would follow through on if she crossed him.

She was a prisoner and so far there was no way to escape him.

The plan was to save enough money and then run for it with the children, and with the money, hopefully she might have a chance to start somewhere new. It was something to hold onto at least, a way to keep her sane. Everyone needed hope, something to look forward to.

At least he didn't sleep with her anymore. That had stopped over a year ago. Now, he went out into the city and fucked hookers and call girls. Though she didn't want him to touch her—ever, it still hurt her pride deep down that he had to go somewhere else to get what she—his wife—should provide him. She didn't understand why she felt this way. She would prefer to kill herself than have him ever inside her again, but still…there it was.

But the children, she had to protect them. They were the only good thing that had come out of her marriage of abuse and pain.

Because she didn't sleep at night, and the stress of dealing with Charlie, Sharon finally slowed her crying, rolled onto the floor in a ball, and drifted off to sleep.

"Mom, I'm home!" her son called out as he entered through the back door and into the kitchen. Rich was twelve, and though he knew his father was far from perfect and saw how his dad treated his mother sometimes, he had no true conception on just how bad it was. His older sister Ruth was seventeen and she had a better idea but didn't know how to stop the pain her mother suffered. Sharon believed if Ruth lived in the house, Charlie would go to her in the middle of the night, and by her not being in the house, he couldn't be tempted, so instead, Ruth spent almost all her time at her friend Wendy's house a few streets over. Sharon was fine with that.

The only time it was hard for Sharon to deal with her life was when she ran into Wendy's mother at the supermarket or the gas station. Her eyes would look at Sharon with pity, knowing what she was dealing with. Ruth obviously shared with Wendy and her mother what was happening in the Thompson household. Wendy's mother would always be cryptic of course, telling Sharon that if there was anything she could do, all Sharon had to do was ask.

Sharon would pretend not to know what she meant and would thank her for allowing Ruth to stay over all the time. The reply was that Ruth was a wonderful girl and was always welcome at her house.

Coming awake, Sharon glanced at the clock on the nightstand to see she'd been asleep for the entire day. Getting up off the floor, she called down, "Hi, honey, I'll be right down," and went to the bathroom to wash her face and clean up. When she looked into the mirror, she saw a middle-aged woman about five foot three, with puffy eyes and a sagging chin, her youth now long gone. She was still pretty for her age, but the constant mental abuse was taking its toll on her. Crow's feet could be seen around her eyes, and there were dark bags under there too from loss of sleep, despite the time she'd just spent sleeping—which was why she'd passed out without meaning to.

She didn't sleep much anymore, too afraid of what Charlie might do at night when he stumbled in drunk. Usually he fell asleep on the couch, but there were a few times he'd come into their bedroom and lay down beside her.

If he tried to have sex with her, Sharon knew that would have broken her to the point she would never come back. Imagine having sex with the most deplorable, disgusting person on the planet and that was how Sharon felt about Charlie. She couldn't stand to be in the same room with him, let alone imagine him ever on top of her, thrusting into her, his sweaty face hanging over her.

Luckily, the few times he would come into their room over the past year, he passed out the second his face hit he pillow. Those times, she'd lay on the farthest edge of her side of the bed, curled up tight in the fetal position, her eyes wide open, her heart pounding in her chest, praying he didn't wake up in the middle of the night.

She preferred the nights when he didn't come home at all.

Straightening her clothes—a casual blouse and a pair of baggy jeans—she wiped her face with a towel and headed downstairs to see her son. As she entered the kitchen, Rich turned to her and smiled. "Hi, Mom, you okay?"

She cleared her throat and plastered a large smile on her face. For her son, the gesture was genuine. Though Rich looked like Charlie, he was totally different in personality and Sharon thanked God everyday that the apple had fallen so far from the tree with her son. He was tall for his age, with broad shoulders and a carved chin. His dark hair fell over his forehead, the bangs so thick his eyes were hidden, and Rich constantly had to brush his hair off his face so he could see.

He was at the kitchen counter, making himself a sandwich when she entered the kitchen. She went to him, kissed his head, and took the butter knife he'd been holding to spread mayonnaise on two pieces of bread. Packages of bologna and cheese were right beside it.

"Here, honey, let me do that for you. Why don't you sit down and tell me about your day," she said and began working on the sandwich.

Knowing how his mother liked to fuss over him, Rich handed her the knife and sat down at the table. "Okay, but nothing special happened today except for one thing."

"And that is?"

"In Science class, Mr. Miller had all these cool and exotic insects that he brought in to show us, and I got to bring home this really cool spider for the night."

She stopped making the sandwich, turning to face him. "Excuse me?" Then her eyes went to the small, clear plastic box Rich was holding after taking it out of his backpack. It was about the size of a shoebox for a one-year-old's shoes and all she could see within it were some leaves and a few pebbles, plus some dirt.

"Cool huh?"

"I don't see anything inside it," she said. "Is that cage strong? I don't want spiders in the house."

Rich laughed. "I don't blame you there, Mom. This spider is special. My teacher said it comes from the rain forest. It's called a nesting spider."

"Oh, and why's that?" she asked, placing the sandwich before her son on a plate. She went to the refrigerator to get him some milk.

"Well, from what I learned in school today, the spider uses live hosts and nests in their lungs. Then it lays its eggs, and when the eggs hatch, the babies come out and start eating the host until there's nothing left but a husk."

"Oh my word, that sounds horrible."

Rich shrugged, as if death was no big thing. "No way, Mom, it's so cool. We watched a video in Science class today where the spider had laid its eggs in a monkey and then how the babies began to eat it from within as they got stronger. It was so cool."

"Not to me, it sounds like a terrible way to die."

Rich shrugged again. "I guess, but hey, Mom, it's the circle of life. At least, that's what Mr. Miller says."

"And why did you bring it home, may I ask?"

"Mr. Miller didn't want to leave them in the school 'cause they shut the heat off at night and the insects he brought in need to stay warm, so me and a few other kids volunteered to bring them home with us."

"Oh, I see, I guess that makes sense."

He picked up his plate and took the glass of milk she handed him. "I'm gonna take this into the living room and eat it there. Is that okay?"

"Sure, honey, go 'head. Just be out of there before your father gets home from work."

Rich's face took on a dark cloud look at the mention of his father. "Yeah, believe me, Mom, I know how to stay out of Dad's way." He stood up and gestured with his chin at the spider cage on the table. "Leave that there for now, Mom, I'll take it up to my room in a bit."

She watched him go, then sat down at the table, sighing heavily. The smile she'd had on the entire time she was with Rich vanished and her normal, harried look returned. Glancing at the clock on the wall, she saw she had three more hours before her husband returned home, that is if he didn't go out and get drunk, which he did almost every night. They had bills piling up because he drank and whored their money away, and there was nothing she could do about it.

Men go to prison, put in a stone box with bars on the windows and bars on the doors, but she bet none of them had ever been in a prison as strong and inescapable as the one she now found herself in.

She couldn't help but think back to when she'd first met Charlie.

He'd been a bad boy even then, but his carefree attitude was what had attracted her to him. He was ruggedly handsome and she had given him her virginity, and in so doing, had cemented herself with him in a way she never could have imagined.

Her mother had warned her, bless her soul. She'd passed on three years ago next month. Sharon's mother had seen the evil in Charlie's eyes but other than a few warnings, had held her tongue, not wanting to alienate her daughter, which can happen when a parent tries to push their opinion on their offspring.

After they were married, Charlie began to change. At first Sharon didn't see it, or chose not to. They say love is blind, and now that she looked back with wide-open eyes, she supposed the saying was true, at least in her case.

When he was mean to her for no reason or yelled at her because his dinner was cold when he came home late from work, she would always rationalize internally that it wasn't him being mean, that it was her. If the food had been hotter she wouldn't have angered him. Or if his favorite shirt wasn't washed then it was on her.

Perhaps it had happened so slowly and had insinuated itself into her psyche because he never hit her, not even once. It had only been with his words and his attitude towards her.

Looking back, she now saw that he was slowly bending her to his will, like a slave master does to a slave and by the time the chains were on the slave's wrists, it was too late to escape.

Her chains were invisible of course, and the threats against her children were stronger than any chains he could hope to trap her with.

"I'm done, Mom, I'll be upstairs doing my homework," Rich said as he entered the kitchen and put his plate and glass in the sink. He picked up his backpack and the plastic cage.

"Huh?" She looked up to see a half hour had passed in the blink of an eye. "Oh sure, honey, dinner will be at six like always."

"Okay, Mom," he said and walked off, his feet clumping up the stairs to the second floor, where his and Ruth's bedrooms were. Sharon's bedroom was on the first floor in the back of the house. She liked it like this. Because the bedrooms weren't on the same floor, the kids had never heard Charlie berate her there. She would always close their door and put the nineteen inch television on so that it would muffle the sound. Then she would sit on the bed and let Charlie insult her and admonish her until he was done for the night and would leave to get drunk with his buddies from work. Of course, he did berate her when the kids were home sometimes, so they did see it happen once in a while. So of course they knew what was going on, but like her, they pretended it wasn't happening. Not that they didn't want to help her, it's just…they were scared of Charlie, too. So everyone acted like nothing was going on, and they all lived silently with a monster.

Standing up, she brushed her hair from her face and got to work making dinner. If Charlie came home on time for a change and it wasn't made and waiting for him, there would be hell to pay.

Charlie stumbled in around nine that night, dead drunk. If the food wasn't hot the instant he came in, she knew he would start on her so she constantly had to reheat it in the microwave, a total of five times since it had been cooked. Of course this would make the food taste not-so-fresh and then she had to worry that Charlie would be angry over that.

As she peered out the kitchen window, she saw his car in the driveway, though the front tire was three feet on the grass. He'd driven home in the state he was in and luckily he hadn't killed anyone. She wouldn't have minded if he wrapped himself around a telephone pole, but the way drunks usually acted, they always took some innocent soul with them, or they came out intact, usually due to being so drunk.

He came in through the back door, barely able to get his key in the lock. Sharon was sitting at the table, her hands before her, waiting. Her stomach hurt.

"Where's my fucking dinner," he slurred while dropping down in a chair, placing his gun on the table beside him. "Damn thing's been digging into my side all night." The gun on the table was more than that though, it spoke volumes to her. She knew it was a warning. "Get me a beer," he spit, burping loudly.

"Haven't you had enough already?" she asked.

He glared at her. "Don't you fucking tell me what to do. Now get me a goddamn beer and my dinner."

She got up and began moving around the kitchen quickly, doing as he asked, her stomach tense with fear. Placing the plateful of food and beer before him with silverware, she sat down across from him. He dug in immediately, shoveling the food in like he was an inmate at a maximum security prison.

"Tastes like shit," he slurred as he chewed and swallowed, barely tasting it.

"Sorry," she whispered.

He glanced at her, seeing her disheveled look. "You look like shit. Would it fucking kill you to look nice when I come home? No wonder I don't want to fuck you anymore."

"I'm tired, I'm going to bed," she said and stood up to leave. As she passed him, he reached out and grabbed her arm, his fingers biting into her skin. She tensed.

"I'll be in too in a bit," he said, then let her go and returned to his food.

She walked away, her stomach so upside down she thought she would vomit. As she walked through the house, she had to pause once and gather herself. In the hallway leading to her bedroom, she tried not to look at the photos on the wall of her and Charlie when they were younger, each of them smiling. A different life that was, one that now seemed like it wasn't hers. Someone else had lived that life and she had that person's memories.

She thought of Rich, who was upstairs in his bedroom and decided to say goodnight to him, so turning, she went to the stairs and ascended slowly, so Charlie wouldn't hear her.

As she walked down the hallway, she passed Ruth's room. The room was empty, which it was most nights.

Music could be heard when she reached Rich's room. She knocked on the door and waited a second, then opened it. Rich was sitting on the floor, playing video games, his cell phone beside him as he talked to a friend.

"I'm going to bed," she told him. "Make sure you brush your teeth and don't stay up too late. You have school tomorrow."

"Dad's home?" was his reply.

"Yes, he's in the kitchen."

"Okay." He never looked at her, his eyes locked on the handheld game in his hand.

"Turn that music down a little more, please. You don't' want to make your father angry."

With a heavy sigh that said, 'parents,' he reached over and turned the volume down on the stereo.

"'Night, honey," she said. "I love you."

Rich grunted in reply.

Closing the door, she went downstairs to her bedroom, to get ready for bed.

* * *

Two hours later, Charlie opened the bedroom door and entered the room. Sharon was still awake, like she always was, and watching TV, though she wasn't actually watching it, just staring at the screen. When you lived with a monster, you never slept until the monster was sleeping first.

The second he entered the room, she could smell the alcohol on him. It leached out of his skin like a living thing. He walked past her without acknowledging her, and after placing his guns on his dresser, he went to their master bathroom. Though the title was pushing it; a small shower, a sink, four feet of space to move around if that, and a toilet were the contents of the 'master bathroom.'

She heard the shower come on and saw the shadows as he went about his business. Her hands were gripping the sheets while she watched. Her attention had shifted from staring at the TV, and now her focus was on the two guns on the dresser. She didn't hear anything the news announcer was saying, as she stared at the firearms.

She imagined Charlie slipping in the shower, cracking his head on the tiles. It would be so anti-climatic if that was how he died. After so much suffering, to have him simply slip in the shower.

Or better yet, she could get up, take one of the guns, go into the bathroom, and shoot him, right there, naked in the shower. She could see it all in her mind, but knew she didn't have the guts. A tear rolled down her cheek and she wiped it away with the back of her hand.

The water in the shower turned off and she heard him drying off, then he padded into the bedroom. He tossed the towel onto the floor, and she saw that despite him being drunk, he was semi-hard.

Oh God, he wants to do it, she thought, horrified. Her mind raced with a way out of it and then she said softly, "I'm having my period." She knew he would never take her if it was that time of the month. It disgusted him to no end.

He chuckled, as if he could see right through her and knew she was lying. Or that's what it felt like to Sharon.

"That's okay, I have a better idea tonight," he grinned and slowly walked over to the dresser and picked up one of the guns, the revolver. The other was a small .22 backup pistol he kept in an ankle holster on his right leg.

"What…what do you mean?"

Did he want her to blow him?

That was as repulsive as having him enter her. The few times he'd made her suck him over the past year had been truly horrific. To make sure she capitulated, he would place the gun to her head while she sucked him. He was a true sadist.

He'd been rough with her, too, slamming his seven and a half inch member into her mouth hard, making her gag. Sometimes she would vomit, it got so bad. But he'd loved every second of it. When he would finally orgasm, he would grab her head tight and his seed would fill her mouth, the salty taste making her want to vomit again. But she knew if she didn't swallow it, there would be more suffering.

When he removed the gun, a small, circular impression was left on her temple and it had stayed there for the entire next day before fading.

She'd worn her hair a different way to cover it so Rich and Ruth didn't see it.

"Come over here," he ordered her as he stood at the end of the bed, an evil smile on his face.

"I'm tired, I want to go to sleep," she said in a whisper. "Please don't make me."

"You're my wife and you'll do what I fucking say. Now get your ass over here…or else." His voice was low and calm, but the threat was there. His member was bobbing as it grew, which told her he was getting more excited.

She closed her eyes for a second and psyched herself up, telling herself she could do this. It wouldn't take long, or so she hoped. Being drunk, it was possible he wouldn't orgasm at all. But she knew if she just got it over with, she could go to sleep and put another day of Hell behind her.

She slid out of the covers wearing only her nightgown, and stood up, then walked to him.

"Get on your knees."

She did as he said, her legs weak and trembling.

"Close your eyes and open your mouth," he whispered, licking his lips. She could see some ejaculate—just a tiny bit—on the end of his penis. She thought to herself that at least he'd bathed before making her do this.

There were times when he didn't shower for days and then would make him suck him. The smell would be terrible and her nose would be so close to him. Yes, this was better. He'd showered tonight. Maybe it won't be so bad.

Slowly, hesitantly, as she willed herself to take the abuse that was coming her way, she closed her eyes and opened her mouth.

But a second later, instead of tasting his warm flesh, expecting his member to fill her mouth, she instead tasted gun oil and something metal was sliding onto her tongue. Her eyes snapped open in an instant and she saw something that almost made her bladder let go but somehow she managed to hold it in.

With his left hand, Charlie was shoving the muzzle of the gun into her mouth as if it was a phallus, while he stroked himself with his right hand.

"Yeah, take it bitch, take it all. Take my cold hard shaft," he hissed and he slid the gun deep into her mouth. "Don't move, slut. My finger might slip on the trigger… and it's loaded.

She whimpered when he said this and looked down to see his finger was where he said it was. She could see right into the chambers and she saw each one was filled with a round. It was so close to her face she could make out every nuance of the metal, from when it had been fabricated.

She began to cry, and as she did, she saw Charlie get even harder. He was getting off on her pain, *feeding* on it, the sick bastard.

"Yeah, bitch, suck it, take it all in," he breathed as he jerked his member harder. She could see the muscles in his arm tightening as he gripped himself, stroking it. He took his hand away, spit in his palm for lubrication, then went back to jerking off.

She was sobbing heavily now, though she knew it wasn't good to do so. Charlie loved it when she cried while he had sex with her. Her mouth hurt, the gun sight on the end scraping her gums and inner cheeks, as he slid it in and out, fucking her hard with the metal phallus, she could taste blood, too.

She began to grow faint and wondered if she would pass out. What would he do to her then, when she was unconscious and helpless? Probably nothing he wouldn't do to her when she was awake, and in fact, he might not want her if she wasn't aware of what was happening to her.

And then he orgasmed, his hot cum hitting her in the face and he thrust the gun into her mouth one last time. Then he withdrew it and she fell forward onto the floor, gagging, sucking in air as she tried to breathe, spitting blood onto the carpet.

He leaned over and picked up the towel he'd used to dry off with and tossed it at her. It landed on her head. "Clean yourself off. I'm taking a piss and going to bed." He walked away from her.

She did as instructed, and when he was in bed and snoring a few minutes later, Sharon hadn't moved a muscle, the towel still covering her head, tasting blood in her mouth from where she'd been cut, her shoulders slowly moving up and down as she sobbed silently into the carpet.

The next morning, Sharon woke up and crawled out of bed. After using the toilet, she went to the mirror and opened her mouth, inspecting the inside. It looked as if she'd been chewing glass. The upper part of her mouth and gums, and the very top of her throat was nothing but cuts and scraps. It hurt to swallow, too.

As she stared at herself in the mirror, she expected to cry but nothing happened. She was too numb to even bother crying today it seemed.

Taking some salt and water, she washed her mouth out a few times, wincing as the salt hit the wounds. She wouldn't be eating anything solid for a while, she figured.

While she dressed, she thought about her life, and wondered how it had become what it was. She hadn't planned on this, that was for sure, it had just sort of…happened.

With a weary sigh, she began her day, which consisted of cleaning the house, laundry and the like. She had to replace the pillowcase she'd slept on because blood had seeped from her mouth while she'd slept and stained it.

When she reached Rich's room, she was pleased to see he was long gone for school. Unlike her husband, Rich was a self-starter and got himself up and out the door every day for school.

Though Rich didn't like her in his room, she always went in and tidied up a bit. Sometimes she thought he didn't even know she did it. She always wondered about that. Did he think elves came in and picked up his dirty laundry off the floor and replaced it with newly-washed items, all folded and neat and placed on the end of his bed? Maybe it was laundry gnomes?

While she was cleaning, she noticed that the small spider cage was still on his desk in the corner of the room. Walking over to it, she examined the cage. The spider was out now and she could see it clearly. It was orange and black and was about the size of her thumbnail. Peering closer, she saw it had wicked looking mandibles, and as she was studying it, the spider suddenly lunged at the cage wall right at her, causing her to fall back and land heavily on the bed.

With her heart beating a mile a minute, she looked at herself and the spider and began to laugh at her silliness. It was slightly forced and an inner voice in her mind told her to be careful. That if she kept laughing, she may not be able to stop, then she would find herself laughing so hard she lost her fucking mind.

Slowly, she calmed down, her laughing becoming a light titter and then nothing at all. Strangely, she didn't feel better after the release and something deep down told her it was because she was becoming dead inside.

Which brought back the ever-present reminder of her husband.

She felt wetness on her lips and touched her bottom lip with her finger, pulling her hand back to see it was blood. She studied it, how it glistened in the morning light. Now that she was more coherent, she tasted copper and swallowed what was in her mouth.

Her wounds within her mouth were bleeding again. Wiping her lips clean with the back of her hand, she got back to cleaning Rich's room. She liked cleaning the house in a strange way. She could let her mind go blank while she did the menial tasks. She began picking up Rich's dirty clothes again, tossing them out into the hall, where she would then gather whatever else she could find from her own bedroom room and Ruth's room, then she would carry it all downstairs to the basement, where the washer and dryer were located.

It was as she was finishing up, and about to leave Rich's room, the taste of blood prevalent in her mouth, her gums pulsing in pain, that she paused before leaving, her gaze falling on the spider cage again.

That inner voice inside was at it again, talking to her, telling her things. Times were desperate, the voice said. What happened last night was a precursor to more terrible things. Who knew what else he might do to her? Last night was a tipping point, last night he had crossed a line when he stuck a gun into her mouth, and if she didn't do something about it, sooner or later he *would* kill her, even if he didn't really want to. It would happen, and she would be dead and her children would only have him.

Thinking of Charlie with the children, and her not there as a buffer, was all it took for her to take a chance, something she would never have done before last night.

She thought back to her and Rich in the kitchen, when he'd first showed her the spider and was explaining about it. *The spider lays its eggs in a host's lungs and then the babies hatch and eat the host from within until there's nothing left but a husk.*

Her mind began working as she thought about those words and what it could mean. Did she dare act on what she was thinking? What if she got caught? Would it even work? All these thoughts flooded her mind, but even as she reasoned this and that, her hands were already reaching out for the cage. With a face void of emotion, she carried the cage downstairs.

When Rich came home from school, the first thing he did was ask Sharon about the spider cage.

"Oh, honey, I'm so sorry but I was cleaning your room and I accidentally knocked it off your desk. It broke and then I stepped on that horrible spider before it could get away."

"You did what? Mom, I need to bring that back to school."

"Why didn't you today?"

He looked ashamed. "I forgot. I totally spaced and forgot it. Now I'm gonna get an F. Taking care of that spider was part of my grade this quarter."

"I'm so sorry, honey. Can I get you a new one?"

He laughed. "Sure, Mom, let's both hop on a plane and go to the Amazon and pick up another one. They aren't sold in the states, they're illegal."

"I don't know what to tell you. I am sorry."

"But you killed it right? You stepped on it?"

She nodded.

"Okay, then it shouldn't be that bad for me. See, Mr. Miller told us about how you can't let animals and insects that aren't part of a locale into a different one. It messes up the ecosystem. But if it's dead that can't happen."

"I see, so we're okay?" She paused and said, "I was thinking maybe you could sleep over Robbie's house tonight? Do you think his mom would let you?"

"I don't know, it's a school night. Why do I have to?"

"I want to be alone with your father tonight."

"Mom, is everything okay?"

She could see the concern in his eyes, and also a helplessness. He was too young to stand up to Charlie, and even if he did, she didn't want to think what Charlie would do to Rich. Sharon did her best to keep the kids as far away from Charlie as possible, and Charlie seemed just fine with that.

"Yes, honey, everything's fine, I just need some alone time with your dad. Could you call Robbie and ask? Please?"

"Fine, I'll be right back."

He went into the living room and she could hear him talking to someone on his cell phone. He came back three minutes later and nodded to her with the phone speaker pressed to his chest. "Robbie's mom says it's fine. She wants to know what time."

"That's wonderful. Tell her you'll be there by five. Does she mind if you eat there for dinner? Tell her I can give her some money to buy you guys pizza."

Rich turned around so his back was to her and quickly relayed what she said, then he turned around and said, "No, it's cool. She's making pasta and there's plenty for me, too."

"Good, so why don't you go do your homework and then you can head over."

Rich said bye to Robbie and slid the phone into his pants pocket with practiced ease. He looked at Sharon, really looked at her, like he was studying her. "Mom, are you sure you're okay? Nothing bad is happening with Dad, is it?"

She put on her best smile, and though her mouth pulsed with agony when she did this, her visage was one of peaceful joy. "No, dear, everything's fine, trust me. Now, you get going."

He stared at her for almost a full ten seconds, and she could almost see the wheels turning in his head as he tried to decipher what was going on with her. But then his cell phone rang and she was all but forgotten. He waved to her and answered the phone, then he was back in his own world of being a teenager, where moms were merely an annoyance.

Ruth came home an hour later but she wasn't staying, she just needed to drop off dirty laundry and get some clean clothes. Before she left to sleep over her friend's house again, she asked Sharon how she was. The two talked for a few minutes and then Ruth left. Sharon could see that her daughter was hurting, but

Ruth's way of dealing was to simply pretend it wasn't happening, that her father wasn't a monster.

Sharon was fine with that. At least Ruth was spared the worst of it all.

A little after eleven that night, Charlie stumbled in drunk and passed out on the couch. Snoring loudly, Sharon entered the room and watched her husband sleep. She could see the bulge under his shirt where he kept his gun and see the ankle holster peeking out of the cuff of his pant leg, where the material had ridden up on him.

As she moved closer, she could smell the alcohol on him, and something else. She could smell the unmistakable odor of *sex*. She stood a few feet from him, watching him sleep, her eyes roaming over his powerful chest, his hard abdomen, his muscular legs. There had been a time when seeing him like this would have aroused her, but no longer.

"Charlie, are you hungry?" she whispered. She wanted to know how deep he was sleeping. Was he really out? Or would he wake up at the sound of her voice.

Charlie snored on, not so much as moving a finger.

"Charlie?" she said again, louder this time.

Still no response.

Walking up and standing over him, she gazed down at the man who had been torturing her for years. But though he looked helpless, she knew she could never raise a hand to him, or perhaps a knife. If she went to the kitchen now and got a knife and tried to kill him and failed, she knew what her fate would be, and unlike her mishap, he would succeed in killing her.

But much like the kings and politicians of old, who would use poison to take out their rivals, as they were too cowardly to try something more violent, she too was about to try something with less risk of exposure.

Turning, she walked back into the kitchen and into the pantry, where she took down the spider cage from the top shelf, where she'd hidden it behind a box of mashed potato flakes.

Taking it to the kitchen table, she donned a pair of yellow rubber gloves she used when washing dishes. She didn't have a dishwasher, Charlie thinking it was a waste of money.

Opening the cage, she reached inside and gently picked up the spider with her left hand, which was visible sitting on a leaf. It curled into a small ball in the center of her right palm when she placed it there. With her heart beating a mile a minute, she spun around and slowly walked into the living room and right up to Charlie, who hadn't moved a muscle. His mouth was open a half inch as he snored like there was no tomorrow. She saw lipstick on his collar and what looked like a hickey on his neck.

She barely noticed these things, however, as she lowered her hand to his mouth and then remained motionless.

What if he woke up right now? That inner voice asked. *What would he think if he sees you with yellow rubber gloves on and a colorful spider in your hand? Do you want to find out? Do it quick, before he wakes up!*

The spider didn't seem interested in moving though and it sat in her palm, still as the dead.

"Come on, go in there," she hissed, shaking her hand a little. But the spider remained motionless.

Becoming desperate, she used the index finger of her other hand and gently nudged the spider closer to Charlie's open mouth. At first it did nothing, but then, when it was a little closer to Charlie's lips and perhaps could feel the warm air he exhaled, it perked up and began to walk. Sharon nudged it in the butt and prodded it closer, and before she realized it, and if she'd blinked she would have missed it, the spider suddenly leaped into Charlie's mouth, to disappear from sight.

Charlie coughed for a second and wiped his nose, before smacking his lips. He rolled onto his side but kept sleeping. Sharon was so scared, she thought she would die at any second, that surely Charlie would hear her pounding heart in her chest like a set of drums, and would wake up. Feeling sick, she turned and raced out of the room.

When she reached the kitchen, she vomited into the sink, and though she did it quietly, her eyes squeezed closed, she found that she felt much better when it was over, though her mouth burned from where her stomach acid had got in her wounds. Taking off the yellow rubber gloves and tossing them to the side on the counter, she ran the water on the tap and washed out her mouth, then sipped some and spit it out. Blood came with it but it wasn't as bad as before; her mouth was slowly healing.

Wiping her mouth and chin with a dishtowel, she tidied up the kitchen, then went to bed.

Days passed uneventfully, and Charlie acted fine, as if the spider had never been put inside him. He was his old self, bullying and threatening her on a daily basis. She could only assume the spider had died. Maybe it had gone down his esophagus and into his stomach, instead of his lungs. It would explain why he was fine. Either way, her plan had failed, not that it was such a clever plan to begin with. After all, what was she thinking? Amazonian spiders? It was something out of a cheap sci-fi movie on cable.

He raped her on the third night after she'd fed him the spider, for some reason deciding he wanted her instead of some whore that walked the streets. It had been terrible. He'd pushed her onto the bed on her stomach and had entered her from behind, thrusting as hard as he could. His right hand had been pressed to the back of her head, pushing her face into the pillow until she thought she would suffocate.

He'd grunted and groaned for almost fifteen minutes, the fact that he was drunk not allowing him to orgasm. But finally, he'd ejaculated inside her, and as he slid out of her and his hand was released from her head, she'd pushed up a little and sucked in air like it was her first breath ever.

He'd leaned over her as she gasped and wheezed, and whispered into her ear, "Next time I think I'll fuck you in the ass. I haven't done that in a long time. Would you like that, Sharon? Would you like my dick in your ass?"

She hadn't replied, knowing that whatever she said would be irrelevant. He'd laughed a little at the thought of what he would do to her and had rolled over and gone to sleep the instant his head touched the pillow. Which was good, Sharon thought. That way he didn't hear her crying, as her will was broken just a little more, and his spent seed seeped out of her, down the inside of her thighs and into the sheet, an ever present reminder of how he'd defiled her.

When she was strong enough to move, she slid out of bed and took a shower, making sure to be as quiet as possible. At least in the shower when she cried, her tears were lost in the spray.

Over the years, Sharon had taken more showers than she cared to admit.

At the end of the second week and Charlie was still fine, Sharon completely forgot about the nesting spider. Her small ray of hope had been extinguished for good and it was back to suffering each day both mentally and lately, physically.

For some reason she didn't know, Charlie was escalating in his abuse. Where before it was mostly mental, now he was becoming repeatedly physical and she knew if she didn't figure out a way to end it with him, she would be dead before the end of the month, if not sooner, and no doubt, so would her children.

But she was too terrified to do anything, so she prayed for a miracle to save her and her children.

A few days into the third week after she'd fed him the spider, Charlie came home a little after three in the afternoon.

"Why are you home so early?" she asked.

At first it looked like he wasn't going to tell her, that it was none of her damn business, but as he flopped down on the couch, he said, "I don't feel good. It hurts to breath so the sergeant told me to take the rest of the day off."

"I'm sorry to hear that. Can I get you anything?" she asked.

"Yeah, a fucking beer, and you can shut the fuck up. I'll be fine, it's probably heart burn."

She went to get him the beer, and upon her return, handed it to him. "Maybe you should go to the doctor," she suggested meekly.

"Fuck you, I don't need some goddamn quack telling me I've got a cold."

"Okay but…"

"But nothing, just leave me alone."

"Okay."

"Hey, where are those two no-good kids at?"

"Rich and Ruth are sleeping over a friend's house tonight."

"Those fucking kids are never here, it seems."

"Yes, I guess you're right."

"Of course I'm right. I'm always fucking right." He finished his beer and threw the can at her. "Get me another one. No, wait, make it two."

She did as he said, not wanting to get him angrier than he already was. As the day moved onward, Charlie drank more until he was good and wasted. A lot of this was due to her plying him with more alcohol to keep him calm. Hopefully, he would soon pass out and she could relax in knowing he couldn't do her any harm if he was unconscious. She was told to sit in an easy chair across from him, *so he could keep an eye on her,* he'd said.

Just before he passed out, he held up the gun and smiled malevolently. "Maybe we can play some more. Would you like that?" he slurred, his eyes barely open. His eyes went to her crotch and he licked his lips. "I bet you need to get fucked." He passed out before saying more. She prayed that when he woke up he would forget what he'd said, as many times he would pass out and not remember what he did or said.

There was no reason to think this night would be any different.

She sat and watched him sleep for over an hour, her eyes never wavering from his still form. The gun was on his chest, clutched in his hand, and once more she imagined herself going over to it, taking it, shooting him, and ending her living nightmare. But if she failed, if she did one thing wrong, it would be her last mistake. She was too terrified to try and she knew she was a coward.

She nodded off a few times and soon it was dark, but each time she would drift off, she would snap herself back awake. She watched Charlie sleep, as if the man was a sleeping tiger and she was afraid to move or risk attack.

After all, he'd said to sit in the chair and if she got up and he remembered the command he'd given her, he might be very angry that she'd gotten up without his permission. But finally, after hours of not moving, her bladder was screaming to be emptied and she decided she had no choice but to get up.

Going to the bathroom was like she'd gone to Heaven, it felt so good, and she figured she might as well just go to bed. If he accused her of disobeying him, she would try and play dumb and say she misunderstood him.

She went to bed, leaving her husband to sleep it off on the couch.

By the time Sharon got into bed, she found she wasn't that tired anymore. Too much filled her head and she ended up just laying there, staring up at the ceiling, for over an hour. But finally, sleep came to her and two hours before dawn, she drifted off into a fitful sleep.

Feeling like she'd just closed her eyes, they suddenly snapped open when she felt something heavy on top of her, pushing her into the mattress. She was laying on her stomach, which was how she usually slept.

It was dark in the room, and she couldn't see the digital clock on the nightstand from the way she was laying. Her lower half felt cold and she realized the blanket she'd been under had been removed, exposing her body up to her lower back, where there was something heavy resting on her back and buttocks. She began to panic, not understanding what was happening.

Disoriented from sleep, she tried to get up, uttering a muffled scream, thanks to her face pressed into the pillow. As soon as she cried out, someone punched her in the left side of the face, rocking her head to the right. Still she tried to fight and received a jab to the kidneys for her trouble. Wheezing hard, the fight was taken out of her and she saw stars.

The weight on her back lifted and she was roughly turned over. She sucked in a breath to scream, but a blow to the stomach stopped it before it left her mouth. The punch to her abdomen made her partially sit up, where she then felt another blow to the center of her chest, before she fell back to the bed. Her mouth was wide open as she struggled to take in air. Drool slid out of the corner of her mouth to roll down her chin and onto her chest.

Delirious from the beating, she was still disoriented and had no idea who was attacking her, or why they were doing it. Then the figure on her leaned forward and down so that their face was only an inch from hers. In that instant, she knew who was on her, who was abusing her. As if there could be anyone else.

The smells of his body wafted into her nose: his body odor, the scent of alcohol, his aftershave.

Charlie.

Panicking, she tried to get up and the back of her head connected with his nose. He cried out in anger and pain as he leaned back, and she tried to get up, only he was too heavy. As she fought to roll him off her, another blow struck her in the side of the face, rocking her head to the side and forward so that it bounced off the headboard, due to her body having been pushed up slightly. White light splashed across her vision and she lay on the bed, partially dazed and confused.

"You fucking bitch," Charlie hissed. "You'll pay for that." He ripped off her nightgown, even though it was already pushed up, and he had easy access to her thighs and what lay between them. "I was just gonna fuck you, but now…" She could hear him fumbling for something on his side of the bed, on his nightstand, the matching pair of the one on her side of the bed. "Now, I'm gonna get mean."

White light filled her vision as Charlie put on the small reading lamp on his nightstand. Then he flipped her over and got on top of her again.

At first she couldn't see, but slowly, her eyes adjusted to the light and she saw Charlie sitting on her stomach with his revolver in his hand, naked as the day he was born. His member was half-erect, and it rested on her chest; she could feel his balls pressing on her skin just below it. He was also sweating heavily and his complexion was deathly pale.

The cylinder on the revolver had been popped open and he shook out the bullets, then picked one round up and slid it back into one of the chambers. Snapping it shut with a flick of his wrist, he spun the cylinder so that there was no way of knowing where the bullet was located. It could be in the next chamber to fire, or it could be in the last.

"Ever played Russian roulette?" he asked, his eyes alight with madness.

Sharon said nothing, staring at Charlie, her heart fluttering in her chest as she became filled with fear. Her stomach and side was aching, and each time he shifted his body, she felt those places flare up with agony. He may have even broken one of her ribs, though she didn't know for sure.

"You don't have to answer. I really don't care." He slowly moved the hand holding the gun and swung it around to his back, then leaned backwards a little. She let out a gasp when the cold metal of the gun touched her thigh, shivers filling her from head to toe. He moved the muzzle over to her inner thigh, and began sliding up to the junction between her legs. The muzzle of the gun tickled her clit ever so slightly, though she felt no sexual sensation from this. In fact, her entire body cringed in revulsion.

He got off her, pointing the gun at her in warning. "You move, I kill you, then I find the kids and kill them, too." He grinned malevolently. "You know I'm not lying."

He slid down the bed and spread her legs apart, and while licking his lips in excitement, his member now fully erect and dripping pre-cum, slid the barrel of the gun into her vagina, fucking her as if it was a dildo. He stroked his member with his free hand, jerking it like it was his first time, his face alive with arousal. She could see he was really and truly getting off on this sadism.

He slid the gun barrel in and out of her in a slow, steady motion, and she cried out each time it entered her. Like before when the gun had been in her mouth, the gun sight was scraping at her vaginal walls, tearing at the membranes and muscles within. She began to cry and let out a loud bark of pain each time he shoved it all the way in, but he didn't stop, and actually began to thrust harder.

He slowed and then stopped with the gun barrel all the way inside her. Blood trickled out of her vagina to seep into the sheets, and it looked like she had been a virgin, the muzzle breaking her hymen.

Charlie hadn't uttered a word as he fucked her with his revolver, his eyes glued to the action as he slid it in and out of her, but now he slowly looked up at her, his eyes locking with hers. He wrapped his hand around the gun handle better and slid his finger into the trigger guard, which was buried in her mound of pubic hair, as the gun was so far inside her.

"So I asked you if you ever played Russian roulette? Of course you haven't, but I bet you know what kind of game it is." He was still jerking his member, sliding his hand up and down on it. "Well, I thought of a new way to play…with your pussy."

As she realized what he was talking about, Sharon's eyes were so wide it was a miracle they didn't simply pop out of her head like a cartoon character. She tried to sit up, but a crack to the jaw sent her falling back to the bed, the room spinning.

"Don't you fucking move, or I swear this will be nothing compared to what I'll do to you," he warned.

He waited for her to become coherent, before he shoved the gun so far inside her that the trigger guard was touching her vaginal lips. She howled in pain, but one look at his face and she slammed her mouth closed, the rest of her howl muffled between her teeth.

"Ready? One, two, three," On three, he squeezed the trigger on the revolver and the hammer came down.

Sharon screamed as loud as she could. She felt the gun vibrate for a split second in her vagina as the hammer clicked on an empty chamber, the click was as loud as a cannon going off. Her bladder let go and she urinated all over Charlie's hand and the gun, but he only laughed harder at her misfortune, not removing the gun even an inch. In that exact instant she screamed, he orgasmed, shooting his cum all over her pubic hair and stomach .

As he let out a roar of pleasure, Sharon's entire body spasmed in abject terror and she felt lightheaded and was very close to passing out, and probably would have if Charlie didn't lean over and slap her face a few times to bring her back to reality. Her cheeks became red from the blows.

"Uh-huh, wakey, wakey, don't you go anywhere, we're just gettin' started," he growled.

She lay trapped on the bed, knowing there was no escape. In that instant, she did want to die, to end it for good. All the pain, all the suffering and mental anguish. Forget about her children, she was going to think of herself for once, and this torture would never end and God help her, she wanted it more than anything else in the world.

She imagined him squeezing the trigger and this time the hammer came down on the chamber with the bullet in it. The round would exit the barrel and enter her body, slice through intestines, her kidney or gallbladder too perhaps, then rip up into her ribcage where it would penetrate her heart and kill her. Then finally, the pain would be over.

But no sooner did these images flood her mind, then reality flooded back in and she thought about Rich and Ruth. What about her children, her babies? Who would protect them?

Charlie began to laugh, but it soon turned into a coughing fit. Even through the pain-induced haze she was in, Sharon saw he was looking worse, though still having fun torturing her. He pulled out the gun. The barrel was wet with her vaginal juices and blood. He spun the cylinder again, then slid it into her yet again, the gun sight once more tearing at her vaginal walls. She howled anew, though this time it was a far weaker showing as she grew exhausted from so much abuse.

When the gun barrel was in over five inches, he began to twist it slightly, relishing her pain as she winced, then he squeezed the trigger. The click of the gun was like an explosion in her ears and Sharon bit her lip, drawing blood, expecting to feel the bullet rip through her insides, but again, nothing happened.

Nothing, an empty chamber.

Sharon's body un-tensed as Charlie slid out the gun. He licked the tip of the gun sight and rubbed it on his mouth, and her blood got on his lips. While he laughed, she sobbed heavily, her hands covering her face as she prayed to be somewhere else, anywhere else in the world but right here with him.

The pillow on both sides of her head was soaked in her tears. He spun the cylinder again and smiled wickedly, the blood coating his lips resembling red lipstick. He coughed for a few seconds and this time it seemed he couldn't catch his breath, but after almost a full minute, he got himself together.

"Okay let's try this again, huh? Man, you are one lucky bitch. Who knew?"

He slid the gun in again and she bit her lip to prevent from crying out in pain. Blood seeped under her to make her buttocks stick to the sheet. Panicking, once again she tried to get up, tried to escape, but a blow to the face sent her falling back to the bed, reeling. Though she may not have been tied up, his brute strength was more than enough to keep her captive. Charlie was almost double her size and could break her like a twig if he so chose.

Her insides were numb from all the tearing within and she felt the gun barrel go into her just barely. But that didn't matter. She didn't know how she knew it, but something inside her told her that he wanted to kill her anyway, and that this time her luck would run out, that he would squeeze the trigger and the hammer would come down on the chamber with the bullet in it.

She could see the muscles in his arms tensing as he prepared to squeeze the trigger, and she said a silent prayer to God to somehow protect her children, that her babies might somehow escape this living monster she'd had the misfortune to marry all those years ago.

Charlie was sweating buckets now, and just before he could squeeze the trigger, he was once more wracked with a coughing fit, one that sent him falling off the bed, pulling the gun out of Sharon as he fell.

The gun came out at an odd angle, the gun sight catching on the side of her vagina before it popped out completely, taking a small piece of flesh with it. She screamed in pain and sat up, more blood splashing onto the sheets.

Between her legs was a throbbing pain that made her feel like she was on fire. She glanced down, not wanting to see the damage, but knowing she had to. Though it was nothing but throbbing pain, and there was no doubt it was bad, she saw that the blood wasn't as heavy as she first imagined, that it was her urine that made up most of what had been under her buttocks and lower back.

Lost in her own suffering and wounds, it took her a few seconds before she glanced down to see where Charlie had fallen onto the floor.

When she did, her eyes went wide yet again, but this time not in terror for herself, but in abject amazement and fear of the unknown. Her hands went up to her mouth as she screamed at the horrendous image before her, her mind trying to accept that the thing on the floor was her husband.

Because weeks had passed uneventfully after she'd put the nesting spider into Charlie's body, she'd assumed it had died, but now, as she stared in horror, she saw that had been the farthest thing from the truth. The spider may have died, but not before having taken up residence in Charlie's left lung, to then give birth to thousands of egg sacks filled with babies. And that morning, the babies had hatched and begun feeding.

Now, a day later, the babies had doubled and then tripled in size, and were eating Charlie from the inside out. They came out of every orifice in his body as he writhed on the floor, his eyes squeezed closed as he suffered in abject agony. As Sharon watched, Charlie's eyelids began to move like something was pushing on them, and then dozens of spiders ate through the orbs, and the eyelids, also, to quickly scurry out of the empty sockets. They came out of his ears, his nose, his mouth, climbing up his windpipe and to freedom. She saw them come out of his anus, swarming over his buttocks to crawl around and drop off to scamper away.

Charlie was screaming at an unbelievable decibel level as his skin began to undulate and ripple, as if the creatures were just under the surface, which they were. His flesh began to crack and break apart, like dried parchment. Spiders swarmed out of the cracks to cover him and yet Charlie still didn't die. He shrieked and flailed, spasming, but he didn't die. He refused to die.

Sharon watched him rolling on the floor as he was covered from head to toe in spiders but still living.

A voice inside her said he was too fucking evil to die. And what if he didn't die from this? What if he somehow managed to live? Surely one of their neighbors had heard all the yelling and screaming and sooner or later a squad car would come to investigate. If the police came, they would get Charlie medical help. They would put him in a hospital, so that he could leach on what finite financial resources they had in the bank. He would waste away and leave her destitute or worse, with mounting hospital bills.

So though she wanted to watch him suffer, *needed* to see him suffer, she slid off the bed, ignoring the spiders she was stepping on, and picked up the revolver from where it had fallen.

Sharon shook the gun gently to brush off the spiders that were on it, then leveled it at Charlie's face as he screamed for help on the floor, his entire body writhing in unbelievable agony as he was eaten from the inside out, organs infested with baby spiders that crawled into every nook and cranny, every space they could find.

The revolver was in the same exact position it had been in when Charlie was about to use it on her, the hammer cocked back and ready to come down on the chamber. From less than two feet away, and with a fire in her eyes that had never been there before, one of defiance and empowerment, Sharon squeezed the trigger on the gun.

The boom of the revolver filled the room, sending it flying from her hand; she wasn't used to the kickback. Then there was no sound except the soft, leaf-like rustle of the hundreds upon hundreds of spiders feeding on Charlie.

Tears filled her eyes as she sat on the bed, but for the first time in as long as she could remember, they were tears of joy.

THE HUNTED

CHAUMA SMITH GUSS

I love the feel of the racing heart, the hot blood spilling across the grass, black and glossy in the moonlight. The hot taste sings through my mouth and into my soul, shivering and bright and crimson. Whoever said blood has a coppery taste or smell has never felt the snap of a hamstring as the prey struggles to flee, never tasted or smelled the lovely rush that comes dark from a slashed throat, never listened to the last gasping breath, a bare mist that shimmers silver against dark leaves.

The hunt was good, filling me up like the full moon above me; three days to stalk, three days to haunt my prey with the knowledge that it was being hunted, and finally, before the moonlight began to fade, the quick chase, the fast kill, and now I am free again. It's poetry to me. Sated, my hunger goes to sleep, a beast that knows one prey. We will sleep, and then I will find the next one before the moon begins its toneless song again.

I hear wolves in the distance and roll my prey into its hasty hiding place. I may come back to visit her, but for now, I am done.

Nick Reynolds slid the form across the desk. "Sorry, Animal Research wants these right now." He tried to look apologetic, but his shy smile made the expression insincere. He squared the corners on the rest of the mail and put it in the basket. His cologne was strong, musk and sandalwood, Mary Hunter suspected it was new.

She glanced at the scrawl and raised an eyebrow. "There are thirty-three periodicals on this request. If Dr. Tucker wants them all 'right now,' then he ought to learn how to use the online form instead of printing it and hand-writing the references." She turned to her computer, smoothly entering the information into the database.

"It makes for a bad Monday morning, that's for sure. At least it's not microfiche." The research assistant, Nick, fiddled with the cup of pens on the counter, restlessly rearranging them until they were all nib down.

"True, or hardcopy." She compiled the articles, saved the file and moved it to the Department Head's folder on the network. "The articles are saved to his directory. I find it interesting that a behaviorist insists on being so difficult about changing his own behavior."

"I don't mind bringing them over," Nick actually blushed and looked down. Mary tried not to smile; smiling only encouraged them.

"No, I guess you don't. Thank you, Nick. Good luck with your exams next week."

He beamed at her as he left. He would graduate in a few weeks and go on to do his Masters' work, probably at the main campus. Then another eager young face would eventually wander into her private territory, find her to be exotic or striking or simply entrancing. According to some of the rather bad poetry she'd sometimes received, she was bewitching.

Every year or so she received at least one angry call from a young lady who was having a hard time attracting her would-be lover from Mary's alluring clutches. Only once had any official complaint been made, and the allegations were quickly dismissed after a call from Mary's own Department Head. She pulled the remainder of the hardcopy requests out of the basket, quickly working through them. The last piece was a copy of next week's Circulation Desk schedule, from the library director. She was mildly surprised to see her name on it. She picked up the phone. "Michael, I just saw the schedule for next week. Do you really need me in circulation?" Listening to his reply, she drew a box in the upper corner of the schedule, quartered it, then drew diagonal lines through all of those boxes. "She's been pregnant for eight months, surely that was enough time to arrange for a temp." Breathing deeply, hearing the edge in her voice, she colored the bottom right triangle in each box. "Sorry, it just gets hectic in Research when I get pulled away. I got another hand written request from Tucker this afternoon." Another box next to the first, quartered. "When do you expect the temp?" The pen stilled. "Three weeks? As long as I can take Ellen in for dialysis on the fifteenth, I can make it work." She fed the schedule to the shredder. "No, thanks, I have an errand to run this evening. Maybe another night."

Passing through the commons, I heard a snippet of a news article; someone had found a body. How very terrible for them. I continued on my way; nineteen days to find my next playmate, nineteen minutes since the delivery was called in, and eleven minutes until the pizza was free. Three playmates found and forgotten—and now perhaps—a fourth before I move on again.

A blonde girl answered my knock, her study group draped across chairs, bean bags and the two narrow beds. They were laughing, and the blonde was too meaty for my taste, not arrogant or bossy, not *the one*. She would be too easy, so I smiled, and took the money, and went for the next pizza, the next delivery. In the parking lot, a woman caught my eye. She wasn't a student, perhaps a teacher. Her hair was a faded brown, wisps curling around the edges of it, falling like a lover's hand against her neck. She was slender and graceful, lean with muscle. She was aware of everyone around her, but pretends to ignore the students upon leaving the library and jostling each other, bumping her elbow thoughtlessly. Turning her head, I suppose she feels me watching her, so I move on. Perhaps she would like to play…

Mary muted the sound on the television and sat down behind the circulation desk. The coverage of the missing co-eds was getting more and more lurid as the week went by. Two missing when the football team was away was one thing, but they had found the body of a third in the woods off-campus the past Friday, apparently killed the week before. The students coming and going in their endless and over-caffeinated search for knowledge were drawn to the reports, drifting closer to any television or radio that might give them that vital piece of knowledge, a bit of wisdom that told them that somehow it couldn't happen to them.

Some swaggered, over-confident with their new tubes of pepper spray on key chains or whistles on lanyards around their necks. It would be less distracting if they didn't all stink equally of fear. Mary squeezed a bit of hand lotion onto the backs of her hands, rubbing it over her wrists and forearms, a haze of vanilla perfume wafting up around her. Most of the students ignored her, even when they brought her their library books. She ignored them equally, scanning the barcodes as the books came back and went out again, focused on numbers and titles, and not seeing them.

Occasionally, one would notice her, would look up, startled into meeting her eyes, smiling at her, fascinated for no reason they could name. She would smile back as maternally as possible, lips closed over her teeth, forcing herself to think about puppies.

By Wednesday, Dr. Tucker tracked her down personally. "Ms. Hunter, where are the articles I requested on Monday?" He stepped close to the desk, looming over her.

She glanced up at him, pushing a stack of books toward the student who was edging away from them. "All requests submitted electronically have been filled, Dr. Tucker."

"I sent my assistant over with the required paperwork two days ago." He was working himself into what he probably fancied was an intimidating lecture-mode.

"Sir, the format for that paperwork changed three years ago," she replied. "Those requests are more efficiently handled when submitted electronically." She debated whether she should stand her ground, and decided it was safe enough. Only halfway through the cycle, she should be able to keep her temper.

He stepped closer to the desk, leaning closer. He wore the scent of a cat on the sleeve of his jacket, the animal claiming him as its own. "Young lady, my research is important work. Several species will become extinct if I do not get the service I require. Can you, or can you not perform your job?"

Maybe fourteen days was too close after all. She looked up at him, meeting his eyes directly. "My job does not…" She paused, feeling *other* eyes on her, the hair on her neck prickling a warning. She stilled for a moment, listening, her gaze still locked with the professor's. He froze under her gaze and she forced herself to look away. "Send the boy with the list," she said. Sweat beaded his forehead. She smelled his unease, and then something else entirely, an acceptable target for her irritation. The growing tension broke and shimmered in the air like heat. Turning towards the main entrance, she raised an eyebrow and then pointed at a man. "You may not," she said, pitching her voice to carry, "bring that in here." The pizza delivery man was staring at them, his expression masked by sunglasses and the red and white ball cap of his uniform. The feeling of being watched intensified. She was being stalked, and she had to fight curiosity and wariness, forcing them down behind her carefully cultivated mask of *librarian's rage.*

"My mistake," he said, and left, the pressure of *other* eyes leaving as well. She was curious, but there was nothing about him that indicated anything other than a man carrying a large pepperoni and hamburger pizza, extra sauce. He was thin, but not tall, and she dismissed him as the stalker. Just a man in a ridiculous hat, she figured.

The distraction restored her control. "Dr. Tucker, please send Nick here with the requests, I'll be happy to fill them immediately when they arrive, barring any other interruptions." She indicated the students lining up behind him and smiled, baring her perfectly white teeth, which were closed.

"He will be here within the hour, of course." The professor was the one watching her now, and he smiled in return until he realized he was doing it and mustered a scowl instead. She accepted the next stack of books and wondered idly if the behaviorist realized why he was smiling, then realized that it wasn't a smile at all, as he retreated back to the safety of his lab.

She was *the one*. I knew it when I saw her so coolly take on the professor, a big man with a big voice and big ideas about his importance. I knew it when *she* felt my gaze and turned to look right at me, pale skin, light brown hair and those pale hazel eyes.

Her voice was clear and crisp, not melodious like some women's voices, not a voice that would crack and strain from screaming.

She was perfect, brave for now. Perhaps, in fourteen days, *she* would survive the hunt, and we could play again.

That was a new thought, my *playmates* should not have to worry about surviving. So, no, *she* would be *the one*.

It would be perfect.

Mary felt the gaze of the *other* twice more that week, once at the library and once again when she was out for a jog in the evening, releasing her limbs from the confinement of being merely human, enjoying the night in a different way as she passed other runners in the park, and then the lovers sneaking away from their Saturday evening studies, their friends or their spouses, trysting in the woods or in the few study rooms in the library with locks. She didn't care about any of it, just the pale sliver of the waxing moon. She turned onto the hiking trail, listening to her soft footfalls and the singing of the wolves in the distance.

When she smelled the kill, she stopped. The body was hidden back in the woods, putrid with the decay of a month or more. Soon the scent would fade altogether. She stayed on the trail, feeling the eyes of the *other*. Raising her face, she stretched casually, every muscle alert, and drew in her breath through mouth and nose, tasting the scent of the kill, rot and bile and insects, ammonia, and the faint chemical undertone of a woman's deodorant, soured with fear. If the *other* was here, visiting this kill, then he wasn't like her.

She disdained killing humans, with their foolish politics and primate grimaces. They preached self-awareness, but didn't even know what their monkey brains knew, baring their teeth and releasing adrenaline when they looked her in the eye, an ape confronted by a predator. They were confused and fascinated; they thought it was attraction, thought her charming, since they smiled every time they met her, and sometimes when they simply thought about her. Harmless Mary Elizabeth Hunter was merely a research librarian. Solitary with her books, periodicals and computers, they never dreamed of the other thing their subconscious sensed.

She noted the spot on the trail and turned back. If she could spoil the site for the *other*, it would move on, having no kill to come back to. Eleven days and she could go herself and hunt. She ran back down the trail, stopping only at an emergency speaker, back in the park, to report the kill site to the campus police. Let the poor things take credit for the find. She would continue on, quietly and carefully, and that would be the end of it.

I bit my hand to keep from screaming with rage. They found another of my girls, filthy pigs rooting through the dirt, touching her, taking her away to pick apart with their TV CSI nonsense. They would cut her open, scrape her body and tweeze away her hair, swab for fluids that would not be there, never there, that's part of the game.

I saw *the one* when I came to visit my girl last night; she paused for a moment in her jog, just to stretch and then turn around. Less than an hour later a fat man in a polyester uniform came with his taser and a flashlight. He went right up to the place where my girl was hidden, and had the unmitigated gall to vomit on her when he touched her hand. I slipped away through the trees, unnoticed, and became just another jogger, leaving as more of the campus 'police' arrived. I was safely gone by the time more serious constabulary arrived.

I looked down at my hand and noticed the blood from my bite; sloppy, stupid, I could ruin everything if I was this weak. Maybe…maybe the new playmate…but how would she know? Of course not, she was beautiful, brave and perfect, but in the end they are all too dumb to see what was truly around them, and only smart enough to sense that they were being toyed with, and as I taught them, they were eventually smart enough to be afraid. That was when the fun really began. But it was over with this poor girl, violated by uncaring people with gloves, cameras and radios.

* * *

Mary recognized the pizza delivery man, wearing his dark glasses even in the grocery store. She paused by the soup aisle, letting him pass her by, taking in his scent and the feel of his presence. She saw him every day now, and wondered if he was foolishly considering her a conquest.

He didn't smell of fear, but of mild excitement, and she watched his posture as he passed, and as she passed him again when he paused at the end of the aisle. He pulled off his glasses and met her stare directly, his eyes dark and hard. He didn't smile, and she looked at him more carefully, not bothering to hide her inspection. A woman with a toddler in tow saw them and steered her cart wide around them, deciding against the perils of the soup and pasta section.

He looked her over, and she realized that this was the *other*. Surprising, sad, he was merely human, but he wasn't afraid of her. His monkey brain was not shrieking and throwing excrement, it was watching her, sizing her up, silent in its cage and ignored. The *other* was stalking her, and the notion struck her as ridiculous. She laughed and moved on, dismissing him, buying fish, greens and cupcakes—she had a silly liking for cupcakes, it made her seem more normal. Who, after all, would be afraid of Mary Elizabeth Hunter, research librarian and lover of cupcakes? The human authorities would find and deal with him. Even if he could hurt her, she was in no danger.

She felt him watch her more often, now. Her awareness grew as the full moon came closer, and sometimes he watched her several times a day. On the tenth, five days from the full moon, she called her sister to verify the times of her treatments. They were not truly sisters, but Ellen Hunter was a kind woman, and knew a little more about the world than most, and even better, knew how to protect secrets. Mary thought about telling Ellen about the *other*, but judged that Ellen—who was five hours away—was safe from his simple predation.

At two a.m. on the fifteenth, as the moon began its final waxing to full, Mary put her overnight bag in the trunk of her sturdy and inexpensive car and left. At seven, she helped Ellen into the passenger seat of the car, left the hospital by eight thirty, and by ten was pulling off an access road.

Time slowed unbearably, and Mary felt the tidal pull of the moon in her bones. A thirty agonizing minute hike and she joined the others—a female like her and three humans who simply believed they were like her—all sitting together. She completed the circle, and the humans sipped, inhaled or chewed the catalyst that let them believe they could be different. When the humans were safely unconscious, she carefully folded her clothes and slipped away from human thoughts, finding the scent of a rabbit with the other female. Silently, they disappeared into the underbrush.

Today is the day, and I bathed carefully, dressed comfortably, and boldly walked into the library. Just inside the door, I paused. *She* was not there. A simpering, giggling, vacuous brunette, nothing like *the one* at all, was flirting with a boy as she scanned his books with the light pen. I went to the counter, not caring if I interrupted them.

"Excuse me," I said politely. They ignored me, and the girl waiting in line behind him gave me an ugly look.

"Excuse me." I was louder this time, and she glanced my way for a second, dismissing me as no one. Slamming my fist down on the counter, they all jumped and everyone looked at me, giving me their undivided attention.

"Excuse me, I'm looking for Mary Hunter, the circulation librarian."

"Obviously, she's not here. Please go to the end of the line and I'll help you when it's your turn." The girl rolled her eyes at the boy she was 'helping' now, and I stalked out. Where was she? Her car was gone from the driveway when I drove past her house this morning. She was not at the coffee shop she sometimes stopped at. She should be here, this is where she worked. How can she play with me if she isn't here?

The beast rumbled softly, deep in my gut, and I felt a flicker of panic. I was out of time, there was no playmate, and the beast was hungry.

Mary met Ellen at the entrance of the hospital on the afternoon of the eighteenth and she drove them to Ellen's home. Ellen talked to her, first in Navajo and then in the white man's language, telling all the old stories about Raven, and the Moon and Coyote, and then telling Mary her own story, adopted sister of Ellen, research librarian because researchers rarely had to talk to people, and Mary loved the stories that the library held.

Ellen told of how they left the reservation where Ellen was born, how Mary's secret self was in danger, even there, where people look for people who are different. The stories grounded her, gave her patterns and purpose for her thoughts, reminding her of who she was and pretended to be. She toyed with the idea of abandoning it all, of just losing herself in the hunt, eternal, but that would have distressed Ellen.

"So you hide where people are all different but all the same, because a college is where people learn how to be themselves, and they don't expect everyone to be like everyone else, even if they're all doing the same things," Ellen said.

"I was watched by a man last time. He thought he was hunting me, that he was learning my patterns, but he wasn't a good hunter. He preys on young women, and I don't think he knows what I am." The words were stiff, as if they tasted wrong, and Mary coughed. "I wasn't going to tell you because you're far enough away to be safe."

Ellen pulled in a breath, holding it a moment as she chose her words. "It's important for you to stay safe, too, Mary. I've been looking for someone new to help you keep your secret. They're doing dialysis twice a month now, and we're running out of time to find a donor."

"That's not what I want. Who else can tell me who I am after I've been moonstruck? I could give you one of mine, I'm almost certain, or I'll find one to give you."

"What a fabulous idea. I'm sure the doctors would love to study your blood and tissues." Mary was grounded again, almost human, enough to hear the fear and sarcasm in Ellen's words, and she bowed her head. "Come inside; let me feed you dinner before you go home."

Mary sat awkwardly at the kitchen table and watched the news through the door to the living room. The *other* had killed again, this time sloppily.

The body was found almost immediately. She snarled softly when the victim was identified, pretty little Tracey Hankins, the temp who had been hired for the summer to work the circulation desk during Gina Lovell's maternity leave.

"Did you know her?" Ellen asked, flipping the fish over in the pan.

"Yes. They're going to put me back on Circulation. Perhaps they'll catch him soon. I don't think I can take another month of checking books in and out. It's just not safe for them."

I can't believe the mess *she's* made. That little girl wasn't worthy, they can have her, they can do their stupid tests. Not enough time, not enough fear, this is a process, after all—that's what they say, the books and the psychologists. They don't know anything. She shouldn't have died so quickly, we still had almost two days left, it wasn't enough, not enough fear, not enough time, the blood doesn't spray as nicely if there's not enough time.

Messy, sloppy, stupid, stupid, stupid. It's *her* fault, changing the rules. Fine. If *she* wants change, we can do change. Another playmate, someone close, twelve days to set the stage, too fast but not so bad, so *she* knows I'm still here, and then—then it will be good. Time to smile, everybody likes the pizza man.

Idiots.

Mary's Department Head, Michael Cates, met her at the back door of the library on Monday morning, leading the way up to her office in Research. Her relief was short-lived. He passed a photograph across the counter top, a still-shot of Tracey Hankins and Nick, Dr. Tucker's assistant, flirting, the *other* standing at the desk next to him. "He asked for you by name, the day she disappeared. Do you know him?"

"Yes, I've seen him quite often lately. I don't know his name, but he delivers pizza for Magic Tower Pizza." Michael had known her and been the Department Head for all of the ten years she'd worked for the university library. Mary suspected that he knew more than she'd told him, but he'd never asked, and she certainly never told.

"Where have you seen him? Just on campus?" His posture was relaxed, but Michael smelled territorial.

"No, everywhere. The grocery store, the post office, several places on campus, and once when I was out running." She stopped, following an instinct that perhaps she was saying too much. She hated the first day back among people; no matter how much Ellen talked to her it was always disjointed.

"He's been stalking you? And you didn't say anything about it?" Mary sat still, silent. "Look, Mary, I know you can take care of yourself. It's important for you to remember that normal women might be nervous or afraid if something like this happens. It's important for you to report this to me, or to the campus police, even the city police. Let me help protect you, please." He didn't look her in the eyes, didn't challenge her. He looked past her ear, as if scanning the horizon. She reached out and carefully touched his arm. He froze a moment, then forced his body to relax.

"Why should you protect me?"

"You're my friend. And because Ellen is my friend, too." Mary wasn't surprised. Ellen said Mary was searching, and Michael wasn't such a bad choice, even if he was a white man and didn't know the language of Ellen's ancestors. Mary tried a moment to remember who had come before Ellen, and only remembered the freedom of running, an echo of another's voice. Ellen didn't have any stories of who came before her. Mary shrugged and stretched, flexing her fingers and shoulders.

"They say that tigers and wolves that are born in captivity and raised by humans are still wild animals, still dangerous even to the humans. How do you know that I won't eat you?" she asked.

He laughed, a little nervous. "I don't. But I do know that you don't consider humans to be worthy prey. That's how you can stand to be with us." This time she was surprised.

"Did Ellen tell you that?" She couldn't remember ever saying that to her.

"No, Dr. Tucker did. He's been intentionally trying to provoke you, but all he ever gets is annoyance or disdain."

"He's studying me?" For a moment she wondered if she was wrong about humans being worthy prey. She blinked slowly and took a long breath.

"No, he's studying wolves. He can be trusted with this."

"Then he can start submitting his requests online, or I'll eat his stupid white cat." Michael laughed, and she was pleased to hear it.

"If they can't find a kidney for Ellen, I'll be there for you when you come back. She told me about when you're moonstruck and what I'll need to do."

Mary coughed, a half snarl, forgetting for a moment that Michael only thought he knew the whole of her truth. "If they can't find a kidney for Ellen, I may not come back. But that's for later. Do you think I should report the *other* to the authorities?" It was a question she would have asked Ellen, and it felt awkward to study his expression as he thought it through.

"Do you want to?" he asked.

"If I was a normal woman and a few days away didn't throw my stalker off my trail, I suppose that would make me nervous and afraid. I suppose I'd call the authorities and my friend, and let them take care of me."

"Good. I should have another temp in to cover Circulation next week," he said.

She growled a little, but like Ellen, he didn't flinch back. She grinned, mouth open and teeth parted, and he grinned in return; his scent was still unafraid.

The pizza is hot, a full five minutes till it's free. Package in the return box, not so hard, next delivery, "Yes, ma'am, that'll be thirty dollars." No tip. I can barely keep the bounce out of my step, it's all so very right. Ten days.

Mary processed the periodicals request on her break. Dr. Tucker's cat would be safe; Nick had entered them electronically for him. Returning to the Circulation Desk, she pulled the box of books returned at the bin outside the Engineering building off the counter and started scanning the books as returned, sorting them onto the cart by category.

A slim envelope was packed in with the texts; she turned it over and saw her name, Mary E. Hunter, in neat letters on the front. She opened it, the garlicky smell of pizza sauce taunting her. The stiff photo paper was tacky in her fingers, the pictures sticking to each other. The photo of Nick, studying in his dorm room alone, was puzzling. The next was even more so, a picture of Gina Lovell, the Circulation librarian, at the medical center with a baby, a man holding the car door open for her as a nurse stood by with a wheelchair. The third picture of Michael Cates and Dr. Tucker drinking coffee at an off-campus café made her wary. She looked inside the envelope again and found a slip of paper. *Which one?* was printed on it.

Stepping behind the filing cabinet and out of sight of the security camera, she sniffed the paper. Faint, smelling of soap and the man's skin, she recognized the *other's* scent. She put the photos and note back into the envelope, then put the envelope into her purse. There would be time for it later.

"If I were a normal woman, I'd tell a friend or the police," she mused, returning the books to their silent shelves. The last of the semester exams concluded that morning, so the library was largely deserted. "But I'm not. He's a hunter of women, of *normal* women. His victims are slender, have brown hair, and aren't meek. If he's hunting them as he's hunted me, his prey would have been uneasy, then afraid. Perhaps he should learn more about hunting."

"Ms. Hunter?" Nick Reynolds was waiting for her at the Circulation Desk.

"Hello, Nick, does Dr. Tucker have another periodicals request?"

"No, actually, I have a request of my own. It's about Tracey."

* * *

As I watch from afar, *she* leaves the library at exactly thirty-two minutes after five, exactly as *she* did before the mess happened. Pausing at the foot of the steps, she tosses something into the trash can, something that *she's* never done before. What are you doing, my pretty darling girl, *the one* I've been waiting for?

I let *her* go, *she* never knew I was watching this time, and *she* drives away, going to the grocery store, because Thursday is grocery day, and trout, salmon, vegetables and maybe a game hen will go into her cart, with milk and sometimes cheese or beef liver. I walk past the bottom of the steps and look into the trash can.

What? Is *she* really so stupid? My hands tremble as I pick up the envelope, her name written on the front. I look inside, and pull the photos out. There are four now. The idiot boy, the mother, the men and—the last was a grainy photo of my last girl and the young idiot boy, standing with me at the Circulation Desk the day *she* was gone, the day *she* betrayed me and I had to take another. I turn it over; written on the back in black ink is my answer. *This one.* My heart beats faster, delighted and enraged all at once. So very easy. Nine days and I would deliver, and the pizza man is always on time.

Mary felt the *other* watching her as she left, and knew that when she drove off, he would not be able to resist her counter-offer. She glanced up into the evening sky at the waning moon. Soon it would be completely dark, a few spare moments when her restless soul was completely still, completely at peace, before the need began to grow again, the need to run fast and far, and hunt, the wind in her face sweet, hot blood and the death struggle, the wild taste of new honey. She made a longing noise, a high-pitched whine not right for a woman's throat. Twenty two days and she would have to run again, and if all went well, Ellen would be with her for a very long time.

The young idiot boy got a job delivering pizza. I almost danced for joy when I saw him, seven days before 'the night.' And the manager was surprised but pleased when I offered to train the stupid lump. I have always been the best and fastest, never late once, on anything. The beast stirred, knowing what was in store for the boy, and I soothed it by planning the next few training days with him, every other night, starting tonight—so very simple.

He recognized me from the library, he's nervous and sweating. Perhaps he'll scream like his sweetheart screamed, that poor half-witted mistake of a girl. As we pull out, the pizza safely in the backseat, twenty six minutes till it's free, I see *her* jogging down the street in the opposite direction. This isn't part of her run, what is she doing? This neighborhood is hardly safe for an attractive woman, even in sensible jogging shoes. A laugh bubbled up in my chest, until I saw her head turn, eyes following us.

Mary glanced up at a quarter after three; Michael appeared from the administrative offices, made a round of the lobby and shelves, poorly disguising his need to patrol.

"You should vary your routine, give or take five or ten minutes, sometimes as much as twenty," Mary advised as Michael returned to the Circulation Desk. They hadn't been able to fill the temp position so sadly vacated by the murdered girl. It was four days until the new moon and Mary was peaceful and serene.

"Am I that obvious?" he asked.

She looked at him directly, and he actually blushed.

"To him you'd be."

"Have you seen him since you came back?" he asked and glanced up toward the security camera.

"He delivers pizza, this is a college campus, of course I've seen him," she said. "Look for the guys in the red shirts and red hats." She started pulling more books out of the return bin. "There's another man I see a lot, too. Four or five times a day, actually. At eight-ten in the morning, and again at eleven-thirty, three-fifteen, and then at five. Like clockwork."

Michael laughed. "Okay, point taken. I'll vary my routine. I'm a little anxious. I wish the cops would find him out."

"Routine is opportunity for a hunter." She smiled a little, and he saw it for what it was, a baring of the teeth, a snarl of anticipation. "Of course, you could simply turn him in."

"Campus police reviewed the security tape and decided it wasn't relevant to the murder. That's the only thing that reveals him that we can share," he explained.

"He will reveal himself, Michael. The hunter will be the hunted, and night will follow day, and the moon will rise again."

"How are you so sure?" He looked more closely at her, trying to decipher her expression.

"The moon always rises, of course," she smiled.

Three times today, I have watched *her* do normal things: the early morning run, the commute to work, a stop at the post office. The idiot boy has tonight off, so I am free to drive past *her* house, to check on *her* evening run, to see the lights go out at ten-thirty, all as usual. *She* sees me at each step of the way, turning *her* face towards me, nodding to acknowledge me. There is something very different about this woman, but of course, there should be. *She* is *the one*, and *she* is perfect in *her* vigilance. *She* will be perfect in *her* fear, too. Four nights, and the idiot boy will be a lesson to her.

* * *

Mary pulled the envelope out of the return bin and opened it. Nick Reynolds smiled at her from the photo, his red pizza delivery shirt and red hat clean and new.

His smile was tight. The scent of the *other* was heavy, anticipation a clear undertone, like the last dampness of a wave against the tide line. She pondered the *other's* choice. The girl was already dead.

The *other* didn't see himself as the prey, and had chosen Nick, who was well aware of what the *other* was. He wanted to avenge Tracey Hankins' murder, so it was easy to bait the trap.

Three days and the moon would be new. Mary puzzled a little over the pace of the *other's* hunt. With sixteen days before the first day of the full moon, he should begin stalking Nick, but Nick seemed to be stalking him. Men were not his usual prey, and she found the *other's* need to report on his progress to be interesting.

She saw it then, the simple plan of the *other*, and sneezed hard, a laugh that Dr. Tucker would recognize from a different sort of throat. Three days and the moon would be new, a dark time when the *other* wouldn't be able to see the blood or the face of his prey.

The evening clerk came on duty and she swiftly went up the stairs to her office in Research, faster than a good runner ought to be able to move. She typed a fast search into the database and saved the articles. At five thirty-two, she exited the library, walking at a normal pace to her car. She stopped at the grocery store, where salmon, fennel broccoli and rice were joined by a half dozen cupcakes in her cart. After all, Mary Elizabeth Hunter was a research librarian, and she liked cupcakes.

Tonight I will be alone, but tomorrow I will feed my beast. The boy thinks he has me, but he's wrong. He will strangle delightfully well, like any other idiot boy who's ever crossed me. No blood, no faces; they don't die for my pleasure, but to satisfy the itch, the urge. Delivering the stupid manling to *the one* would be the delight, to see her cool disrespect evolve to fear. Oh, her fear will be quite ripe by the time the moon calls for it.

She arrives at work just as she should, on time and with little fanfare. She glances my way and smiles with a brief baring of teeth. I resist the urge to smile back, to acknowledge *her* greeting, but my heart beats a little faster, my breath catching in my chest. Yes, *she* will be a very good girl.

The day before the new moon was a long and sleepy summer day. At ten in the morning, just before her break, Michael appeared with a man in a plain dark suit and a student intern. "Jason will handle the Circulation Desk for a few minutes, Mary, we need you to answer a few questions," he said.

Mary nodded obediently. "Jason, you may scan in the books and scan out the books, but please don't sort them."

The student nodded and stood aside as she stepped out from behind the massive counter. Mary followed her Department Head and the stranger to the conference room. She could smell the leather holster and gun the stranger carried, but he was merely interested, not suspicious. The men waited until she seated herself, her back to the door and to the left of the head of the table; things they would see as vulnerable and non-dominant. The stranger sat across from her, and Michael took the chair at the head of the table.

"Mary, this is Detective Steve Smith, he's been looking into Tracey's murder." She shook the detective's hand gently, meeting his eyes briefly and then looking away, very careful not to spook him.

"How can I help?" They had found the search she'd initiated last night, a cross reference of female disappearances and deaths and male disappearances and deaths on calendar dates corresponding to the full and new moon.

"We need to know more about an information search you launched yesterday. Who initiated that particular periodical request?" the detective asked.

"It was a personal line of inquiry, not a third party request." Mary looked from one to the other. "I didn't find anything I felt was relevant, but it's also outside my field of study."

The detective made a note. "What do you do for the library?"

"I'm a research librarian. I process faculty requests for periodicals and bibliographies. Currently, I'm also temporarily serving as the Circulation Clerk, while the regular clerk is on maternity leave." Another note.

"Do you often pursue your own lines of inquiry?" he asked.

"Only occasionally, when I find something particularly interesting. Last month, I did extensive research on Ethiopian Christianity, specifically the group that claims to have possession of the original Ark of the Covenant, and last year a request came in regarding seasonal festivals and lunar festivals in Peru, so I spent some time pursuing that." She looked down at her hands, making a point of rearranging them nervously, then glancing at Michael before looking down again. His expression was interested, but otherwise closed. "There's a show about criminal profilers on TV, I was curious to see what a profiler might find if they did a media search on the recent local murders," she said.

The detective stopped writing and raised an eyebrow. "And what did you find?"

"The parameters didn't reveal anything I saw as terribly important or statistically significant. I looked back over the past nine months of the academic year. Four girls have gone missing in the past four months; two of them were found murdered and disposed of in shallow graves in the woods on or near the campus. The other two haven't been found yet. They tend to go missing on the first day of the full moon, but they're never found until after the last day. There were no details on how they died, so I can only assume it may have been gruesome. The second line of inquiry was on male students who have gone missing, there were three, only two deaths; both were prior to the first female disappearance. Both bodies were found on the day after the new moon, and both deaths appear to have been by strangulation. I suppose they were muggings." She shrugged. It was just data to Mary Hunter the Research Librarian. Behind that mask, though…

"What do you mean by the first day of the full moon?" the detective asked.

Michael shifted a little, looking bored and uneasy. The detective was interested now, though he pretended to be bored.

"The moon appears to be full for three nights. Most people just can't see the slight missing sliver on the first and third days. It drives astrologers nutty, and that's why sometimes almanacs show the full moon on different days," she explained.

The detective looked off into space for a moment, tapping his pen against the paper. "Thank you, Ms. Hunter, for your time."

"Not a problem at all, Detective Smith. I'm just sorry I wasn't able to give you better results." She stood. "Are all of the research queries monitored by law enforcement?"

He shook his head. "Not quite like that, no. This case is sensitive, though. Please don't discuss the results of your research with anyone."

She left the room and relieved Jason, sending him on his way. A few minutes later, Michael came back to the Circulation Desk. "Don't do anything stupid, Mary." He was angry and afraid.

She shrugged. "It'll be all right. They'll find him more quickly now."

"Launching a query that you know would flag to law enforcement databases isn't a good way to stay low-profile."

"People who are always low profile in everything they do, who are never noticed, are the ones who are noticed the most when a search happens for people with something to hide," she said.

He laughed a little, taking a deep breath. "You make my head hurt." He rubbed his face with his hands.

She produced a single-dose packet of Tylenol from a supply drawer in the Circulation Desk. "If your headache doesn't feel better shortly, please go to the clinic in building four." She flashed an open mouthed smile at him before pulling out the bin of returned books.

Today is the day. The idiot boy's shift starts at four, and we finish at midnight. Midnight is such a nice time of night, not the witching hour, but somehow just as satisfying.

Six runs, then seven and eight, all under twenty-five minutes, some decent tips, too. The students are celebrating summer, every one of them. The night is dark, so dark. Eleven fifteen, and we're sent out on a final run, his final run. I let the idiot boy drive, and he takes us through the familiar streets of darkening houses. I am so caught up in my enjoyment of the night that I don't recognize the driveway we're pulling into until I see *her* car.

Really? So delightfully symmetrical, that *her* home would be the last home the idiot boy visits. But there is an SUV in front of her house, parked on the street; the tan vehicle her supervisor drove. Interesting, very interesting—perhaps there will be more play than I thought in this.

"Do you want this one, or do I take it up?" The idiot boy was eager for the tip, he'd gotten greedy tonight.

"We'll both go this time, last delivery and all."

Mary and Michael both answered the door.

"Nick!" Mary exclaimed, locking eyes with the *other* as she spoke with the boy. "How good to see you. Is this your trainer?" She smiled at the *other*, teeth bared and closed.

"Sure is, he's the best," Nick grinned.

Michael paid Nick for the pizza, a healthy tip included.

"It's so good to see you together tonight. Drive carefully, it's getting late, and it sure is dark," she said.

The *other* flushed red, a vein pulsing in his temple.

"This is the last delivery of the evening and my last day of training. Ms. Hunter, I got the test results back, I'm a match for Ellen," Nick said.

Michael gave Nick a puzzled glance, and then gently touched Mary's shoulder. She turned away from the *other*, offering her back to him with clear contempt.

"Congratulations, and good luck, Nick. I know that Tracey would be proud." Mary was calm, almost cheerful.

"Wait." The *other's* voice was tight, almost strangled. Mary turned back to them and Nick shrank away. There was nothing human in her expression, in the eyes that were less hazel than feral yellow. "Don't you value this idiot boy's life?" he asked. "Don't you fear for him?"

Michael finally saw the knife, though Nick still seemed unaware. Nick was backing up until the *other* easily grabbed him, twisting an arm behind his back, and pressed the knife to the boy's throat.

Deliberately, he pressed the knifepoint against Nick's bare skin, and blood welled up beneath it. Mary's nostrils flared at the scent, and the other watched her, fascinated, even as he also inhaled the hot smell.

"Are you stalking him for me, little hunter?" She blinked slowly. "Do you think that he's your prey?" She stepped forward, ignoring Nick's grunt as his wrist was pressed more savagely upwards.

"I'll kill him in front of you, and then I'll do the same to your boss, and then, little girl, you will be mine." He licked his lips, lust and rage fighting for dominance as he watched her.

"What fun is that?" She reached out with a finger and touched Nick's blood, suddenly much closer to her, and delicately tasted it. Nick swallowed, hard, and closed his eyes.

"There's no sport in taking prey that is tied up like a goat set out to bait a tiger," she said. "It's far more…satisfying…to hunt, to chase it until it tires, to confuse it until it turns back on itself, its heart thrumming with fear. Do you know the feel of a hamstring, taught beneath your teeth, and then the wet snap when it's torn?"

She pulled Nick away from the *other* and stepped in just as close, the knife between them, inhaling the man's scent through her mouth and nose. "Little hunter, I know what you're hunting, I know that it's me, and that little girl Tracey and those other girls. I know that you hunger for the pain and the fear and the kill, and that if a little girl isn't enough, that you'll kill a little boy by the dark of the moon. Always the dark of the moon, and little boys, always strangled, never bloody. You don't want to see their faces, you don't like that they arouse you just as much as the little girls, and you can't bear the thought that you're less a man because you want to sink yourself into their hot and bleeding flesh, too."

The *other* was trembling, rage and joy and an ugly desire in his expression.

"You want to hunt me, even now, because this little boy's blood, so hot and sweet, isn't enough." She moved away smoothly, beyond him and into the black of the night, turning him away from Nick and Michael. Her eyes gleamed silver in the porch light. "Come and get me." Then she was gone, the *other* following after her into the woods with a wordless cry.

This, yes, finally, *she* is *the one*, there can be no other. How sad that I will not see *her* blood spray across the grass or leaves.

How sad that I will never hunt *her* after this, that all other kills will pale in comparison.

How lovely is the night, with the sound of *her* breathing and footfalls ahead. *She* has stopped. It's disappointing that it's over so soon, especially after *her* little speech. A few steps more and I find a pile of clothes, still warm from her body, shoes damp with dew.

I hear a low moan nearby. Perhaps she has hurt herself, but then it rises into a mournful howl, wolf-like.

I listen to the silence that followed, and a bare whisper of leaves brings slashing pain in my calf. I bring my knife up as a heavy weight bears me down, hot breath, slashing teeth, eyes glowing in the faint light of the stars.

The idiot boy's blood mingles with the blood of the beast on top of me. The knife slashes down and across as *her* teeth sink deep into me, ripping my shirt, then my belly, and finally closing on my throat. I embrace *her*, the knife falling away.

I can feel that *he*r fur is covered in blood, my blood, and *she* is beautiful.

Michael waited on Mary's porch, the phone and a cup of coffee on the railing beside him, Ellen's rifle and a blanket lay across his lap. Nick waited with him, a band-aid over the small cut on his throat.

The police were long gone, now searching for Mary, hoping that the killer hadn't finished his work. Wolves were heard in the night, and Michael had suggested to the eager reporters that they contact the head of animal behavioral research, Dr. Tucker.

After a time, they had left, too. Pre-dawn was glimmering in the east when the waiting men saw Mary lope up across the grass, her body and hair streaked with blood, a slash across her shoulder and ribs. She held something carefully in her hands, close to her body. She sensed them on the porch and stopped, nostrils flaring as she raised her head. Michael set aside the rifle and stood slowly, shaking out the blanket. She hesitated a moment and then stepped close to let him wrap it around her, covering her, holding her against his body as they eased down to sit on the steps.

"It's all right, sweet Mary, you've come home," Michael said softly so Nick couldn't hear. "Ellen tells me I have to tell you stories, get you grounded again. Then we'll call the police again, and be normal people reporting a heinous crime. Then we'll go see Ellen, together." She brought her cupped hands up, opening them. Michael swallowed hard when he recognized what she held. He barely managed not to vomit. "Oh, honey, I'm sorry, but Ellen can't use his kidney, and we have to put that away somewhere before we call the police."

"That's not for Ellen. It's for me, and for Tracey," she said. "Ellen will get one of mine." Nick walked over, holding out a trash bag and she dropped the kidney in it and turned away, pressing her face into the blanket. "Surgery's scheduled for next week. Thank you."

She looked back at Nick, nothing of human understanding in her yellow eyes. He ducked his head, looking down at the ground, and left them.

OCCUPATIONAL HAZARD

MARC SHEMMANS

In the social hierarchy of vocations, journalists are generally regarded as vermin, way down at the bottom of the moral ladder somewhere between lawyers and traffic wardens.

It didn't matter that Cooper was an honest young man, that he genuinely wanted to publish stories that helped and informed. For every eager interviewee or polite local, there was someone who regarded him with marked distrust or loathing. Many people didn't see him as a well-meaning junior reporter—they saw a sly predator, waiting to chew them up and spit them out. His profession was tainted; those tabloid sharks on the red tops certainly had a hell of a lot to answer for.

Cooper sat in his car with the photos of the gruesome murder splayed out on his lap. The poor girl had been ripped open. Stacey Burrows, sixteen-years-old, raped and shredded. The photos depicted a corpse lying face-down in a puddle of blood, waves of rippling, thick blond hair blanketing her face. Her skirt had been pulled up around her waist to expose her bare, pale buttocks. The killer had violated her after her death.

It didn't matter how much serial killer research Cooper studied to prepare himself. He couldn't understand how anyone could hurt something so innocent and pure. The girl had her entire life ahead of her. What did she do wrong?

With persistent investigative journalism, another brutal murder could be prevented. The killer might be caught, if Cooper was good enough.

The journalist sighed and placed the photos back into the envelope. He stepped out of his car into the broad sunshine. The day's light seemed surreal; the neglected neighborhood with its abandoned houses and vast stretches of silence seemed a world that belonged to shadow and darkness. Stacey Burrows lost her life here; she'd been a pretty girl who lived in an area where violent crime was the norm. But Stacey hadn't been murdered for drugs or out of jealousy. She was a quiet girl who stayed out of trouble and dedicated her hours at home to completing homework. Stacey didn't cavort around with troublesome, lusty boys.

Someone afflicted with a terrifying sickness had deprived the world of her potential.

Cooper had a very short list of people who might be willing to contribute to his story. He walked down the block and found the house that he was looking for. The street's peaceful breeze, complemented by chirping birds, couldn't dispel his sense of foreboding.

He glanced around at the boarded-up windows of derelict houses. A couple of rough, hard-faced youths glared from across the street. He'd heard of colleagues being chased away from the area before. Nervous wasn't the word.

The man who answered the door seemed to be one of the doubters. Cooper was not an intentional snob, but his middle-class sensibilities couldn't help but be wary of the man's tattooed neck, thick, gruff accent, and broad shoulders. He was about forty-five, Cooper reckoned, and looked like he could handle himself and more.

"What do you want?"

Cooper politely introduced himself as a reporter from his paper, the large daily based in the city center.

"I'm sorry to bother you. I just wondered if I could ask you a few questions about what happened here last week."

The man grunted. "You mean the murder."

"Yes."

"We've had plenty of your lot 'round here," said the man, regarding him with curiosity. "That was mainly the first few days, though. Spoke to a couple myself. Why are you here?"

"Well, the police haven't caught anyone, so I'd like to ask how people here are feeling about it. Whether people are worried. I'm sorry." He extended his cold, clammy hand. Your name's...John Sullivan? I'm Tim Cooper."

The man shrugged and stared at his hand. "Flogging a dead horse aren't we?"

Cooper shuffled uncomfortably on the doorstep. It was true in some respects; after the first few days of coverage, there' been few developments. The killing was initially a front page-worthy slaughter, but after the appeal and the obligatory tribute piece, the only real peg now was that someone was still at large. There had been no arrest. The police were getting impatient. The nationals had initially covered it, but now there was fresh political intrigue and a couple of shootings in London for them to look at. Cooper's news editor had sent him along to try and get a good page lead—the usual 'Climate of Fear' or 'Residents Blast Police' line.

Cooper cleared his throat and said, "I'd understand if you don't want to talk to me."

Sullivan tilted his head to one side and thought for a moment. "Well," he said slowly, "I haven't got much on till this afternoon. You want to come in?"

Cooper was surprised—he didn't know how to respond. The man gave a wry smile and took a step back.

"We're not all dickheads 'round here. And I didn't know the girl well enough to be pissed off by all your questions."

Cooper nodded rapidly. "That's great. Cheers."

"No problem. I reckon those lads out there might have a go if I don't let you in, anyway."

Cooper's smile faltered.

Sullivan laughed. "Come on in then."

He gestured for Cooper to cross the threshold and closed the door after him.

The hall was dingy and musty, with muddy footprints on the dark, worn blue carpet.

There was a steep staircase to the left, what looked to be a living room to the right, and a door straight ahead at the end of the corridor.

They walked into a small, clean kitchen. The walls were peeling and there was a noticeable draft, but it was pleasant enough. There was a table in the corner with a couple of wooden chairs, and the host gestured for his guest to sit down.

"Tea?" Sullivan offered.

"Oh, yeah, that'd be great, thanks."

Sullivan put the kettle on and turned to face Cooper.

Cooper took out his notepad and pen from his jacket pocket and put them on the table in front of him. The margins were already drawn on the left-hand side of the paper, and he flicked out the nib of his pen to take down good quotes. It was an instinctive practice. Sullivan raised his eyebrows.

"Always used to think you guys used tape recorders and that," he said. "I saw that most of the other reporters who've been 'round here took notes, too. Seems a bit old fashioned to me."

Cooper nodded. "I know, but shorthand is really useful. If you're good, you can get everything down. Technology can always play up on you."

Cooper began. "Can I have your surname and age please, just for the record?"

"Sure. It's Sullivan. I'm forty-one."

"You have children?"

"Two kids, both in school at the moment. They live here with me. I'm divorced."

"Okay."

Those details were printed in longhand at the top of the first lined sheet. Cooper drew an opening quotation mark beneath them. The kettle boiled and Sullivan turned and made the tea before handing one of the steaming mugs to Cooper.

The trainee sought the best opening gambit.

"You said you didn't know Stacey Burrows well, but you did know her?"

Sullivan, who remained standing, shook his head. "Not really. Didn't know her or her family. Seen her around. She was a good-looking thing."

"What did you feel when you heard she'd been killed?"

"I was shocked," Sullivan took a deep sip from his black tea. "Who wouldn't be? You get a lot of bad stuff going on in this neighborhood, lots of kids breaking stuff, some fights, loads of drugs, but it's been a while since anyone got killed. And the *way* she was killed...in her own home. Sounded bad."

Cooper recalled the gory photographs. Sixteen year-old Stacey Burrows had been discovered upstairs in her bedroom, covered in blood, opened up with a knife in a dozen places. Her death was a terrible blow to an impoverished community. Did the killer live in the neighborhood? Could Sullivan's children be in danger?

Strange symbols danced with the motion of his pen across the page.

"Did you feel anything else?"

"You want me to say I'm scared — worried — for my kids?"

"I'm not here to put words in your mouth."

"Look, some people are scared. Those who knew her are in pieces, and angry — it's probably best not to doorstep *them*."

Cooper knew the Burrows family was currently staying with relatives; the police had asked for the press not to bother them.

"Yeah, some people are angry," Sullivan continued. "Some people are sad, and a few people probably don't give a shit, but a lot of people are worried. Some people, like me, don't know what to think."

Cooper nodded, still taking notes.

Sullivan raised his eyebrows. "Am I not helping enough?"

"Oh, no," Cooper quickly said, eager not to seem ungrateful or rude. "You've been great."

His host didn't seem to be convinced. He leaned forward and spoke with blunt sincerity.

"Look, a lot of people are shocked about this. Young girl gets raped and stabbed, and even if you didn't know her, people feel it. It's a bloody terrible thing. We'd all like to get our hands on whoever did it—I've a daughter of my own. You just look at the flowers outside her house, by the police tape, and you can see how horrified people are about what's happened. Sure, they're sad, but a lot of them are afraid it could happen to them, to their kids. In a way, you could say it's united quite a few people. United them in fear."

Cooper blinked and looked up. He'd been writing that down—it was amazing what people came out with. Everyone was so media savvy these days they practically spoke in sound-bites. It might be interesting. Community united in grief by tragedy, perhaps?

Sullivan said nothing for a moment, but downed the rest of his tea. He licked his lips, examining his guest closely. "There was a phone call. I was at the Burrows house when the cops showed up that first night. There was a crowd of us out there. My daughter, Jenny, started to cry. Stacey babysat for me a couple of times. Like I said, she was a nice girl, got along real well with my kids. She put an ad in the paper a few weeks ago so I called it."

The father looked away, clearly uncomfortable. Cooper's pen scratched away furiously.

"Like I said, there was a phone call that night. I shouldn't even have answered it. Breathing on the other end. There was a voice. A man. He said that...Jenny is real pretty. He hung up after that. I answered it because the number...was from the Burrows house."

Sullivan suddenly turned back to Cooper, his eyes red with fresh tears. "I need you to leave. There's nothing else for you here."

Cooper thanked Sullivan for his time and left. He handed him his card in case he wanted to get in touch, and added the man's number to his contacts book should he need to speak to him again.

Outside, the temperature had dropped significantly, and the two youths had vanished from across the street. It was deathly quiet, and the sky was a miserable gray.

Cooper elected to return to the office and finish his story there. He'd tried four houses after the conversation with Sullivan; there'd been no answer at three and a swift rebuke at the other. He had no desire to go digging further.

As he made his way back around the corner of the street, he prayed that his unremarkable car would still be there unharmed. He sighed with relief when it came into view and was pleased to see that there was nothing obvious amiss.

Wasting no time, he drove straight back to HQ and strode into the bustling hub of the main office twenty minutes later. A glance at his watch told him it was still an hour or so until his preferred lunch time.

The open-plan office was set in a large, high, brightly lit room, with a maze of desks arranged in a spiral from the outside into the center.

Cooper passed the sports desk and the blaring sound of live cricket from TVs above. When he arrived at the news desk, Bob Banks, the news editor, was involved in an animated discussion with his deputies. Cooper waited patiently for his turn. His ears were full of the sound of tapping keys, ringing phones, rapid voices, and the occasional curse or hiss of frustration.

Bob finally turned to Cooper with his trademark, stoical expression. "You have fun out there this morning?"

Cooper smiled. "I got some decent quotes from one of the residents. I can get the story written up pretty quickly."

Bob was a balding, middle-aged man whose recent divorce left him with too much time on his hands. He was a private man, but the story went that his ex wanted kids, and he didn't. The man never seemed to leave the office.

"Is there a decent angle?" Bob asked.

"I'm thinking something along the lines of, 'Community United in Fear as Killer Remains at Large.' I think it could work."

"That sounds good. Nicely done. Three hundred words by this afternoon, please."

"It's a bit sad, but I can make it less...morbid."

Bob was already shuffling through his papers for something else of interest. "Sad?"

"The girl was only sixteen. The killer defiled her afterward. They can't get any info on the semen...it's as if the bloke who did it never existed."

"Maybe the girl was a tease," Bob shook his head and pursed his lips and quickly changed his tone before Cooper could interject. "You should think before you talk, Cooper. You're not a cop. They likely already have a few suspects, and besides, there's always mayhem over in Halton. The killer's likely nothing more than a rejected misfit. We move on to the next story—there's always something else. To work now, Cooper."

Bob's eyes finally glanced up at Cooper. His cold glare suggested that the conversation had run its course lone ago.

He went to his desk and sat down, greeting a couple of his nearby colleagues as he did so.

Cooper gave the computer in front of him his complete attention. He laid his note pad onto the desk and skimmed through to find the quotes he wanted. Deciphering his shorthand, he began to type out Sullivan's words, ordering them into clear, tidy sentences.

With the first draft written out in twenty minutes, he spent half an hour tinkering around with it to get it right. He was relatively happy with the end result—it wasn't exactly a work of art, but it would do. Bob had already emailed him additional assignments, and he didn't have all day to sit around perfecting it.

He saved the file and dropped it into the electronic news desk basket. He expected it to get chopped and changed a little bit, but hoped it would still make a page lead.

They hadn't heard when the funeral of Stacey Burrows would be, or whether the coroner would be releasing the body anytime soon. When the funeral or memorial service happened, that would be a story for sure, but he doubted he'd be picked to cover it.

Cooper checked the time and decided to get himself a sandwich. He'd eat it at his desk, as per usual, and then get started on his afternoon's work.

Besides the unsettling interview with Sullivan, it was a normal, run-of-the-mill news day.

In the evening, and finally back at home, Cooper kicked off his shoes, flung off his jacket, and collapsed in a chair. His housemate wasn't home yet.

He watched TV, ate a bowl of pasta, then went upstairs for a shower and changed. His housemate called to say he was out at the pub, but Cooper declined to join him.

More TV as the hours wore on. Boring reality shows. Atrocious makeover garbage. A documentary on Channel 4 about a half-ton woman was promised tomorrow.

Later, his phone rang.

The mobile buzzed in his pocket. He retrieved it and looked at the glowing green display.

He didn't recognize the number, but it had a local code. Instantly, he remembered Sullivan's story. He convinced himself that it was stupid to be afraid, and he would answer the call to prove it.

"Hello?"

He heard what sounded like static, accompanied by a muffled crackling on the line.

"Hello?" he repeated, louder this time.

Still it crackled. Not an obvious prank call. Perhaps a wrong number, or just a bad signal?

The call ended abruptly and there was silence in his ear. Cooper checked the display, and a few moments later, he called back.

It rang out. No voicemail. Just an endless chirp.

Cooper stowed the phone back in his pocket. After thinking for a few moments, he opened his contacts book and flicked through to where he'd registered Sullivan's details.

He checked the home number he'd taken down and was pretty sure it was the one that had just rung.

He took out his phone again, checked the call log, and saw that he was right.

He groaned.

At this late in the evening, tomorrow's paper had already gone to print; he really hoped that Sullivan wasn't calling to say he didn't want to be named, or worse, that he didn't want his quotes included after all.

Cooper tried calling back a second time, but again it rang out. There wasn't much he could do. If it was important, he was sure Sullivan would ring back.

The next day, Cooper's article sat mostly untouched at the top of page five. It was unaccompanied by a photo; a picture story about a new council initiative to stop litter louts provided the visual flair, boxed-off to the side and underneath.

Gillian had returned from holiday. Just two years older than Cooper, she had also been a trainee till she passed her NCE last month, and was now a fully-fledged reporter. She'd been great with help and advice, and was lovely to be around. She breezed into the office that morning, all smiles and flicking, highlighted hair. Her ten days in the sun had gifted her with a healthy tan.

"How's it going?" she called, slipping into her chair directly opposite after a brief chat with Bob and some of the others.

He smiled. "Not bad. Not been the same without you, though."

"Aww, thanks," she said, laughing. "Did I miss much?"

"Oh yeah," he said. "Teenage girl was stabbed to death last week—her corpse was...well, you can read it. No one's been caught. I went out there yesterday to talk to people about whether they were frightened, that kind of thing. It was out in Halton. I went there myself yesterday and interviewed a bloke."

"Bloody hell," she said, her face contorting. "Some people are just animals. Always amazes me when you hear about stuff like that. I was in Halton just a month ago."

"Really? For what?"

"Bob sent me out to do a piece on urban decay. What'd you say the girl's name was?"

"Burrows. Stacey Burrows."

"Name's familiar...is your article in today's paper?"

"Yeah," he said, offering her a copy. "Page five. We've been covering it since it happened."

Most days, the police line had details of a fresh robbery, rape, and occasional murder to write up for the following morning's edition. The city had its fair share of low-lifes, crooks, and psychos. You could see their exploits set out every day in neat print and images in the pages of the paper or on the local TV news at night. Nasty things. Callous things. The choice of what to give more column inches, or any column inches at all, was a key one.

The Burrows girl had been a striking case because she was young, she'd been raped after her murder, and the killing had been so gruesome. Around the same time, a middle-aged man had been killed in a brawl outside a pub, just miles from where Stacey Burrows had been carved up. Victim not as sympathetic, method of dispatch not as gory. That story had been included on page six, tucked beneath a report on a tasty sexual harassment employment tribunal. In news, one life was never going to be worth the same as another.

Gillian finished reading his article and looked up. "I did an interview with the Burrows girl. Caught her outside playing with a little boy...could be Sullivan's boy. Sad. Nice story, though."

"Cheers."

"Must be hell for the family," she shook her head. "I've done death knocks, and sometimes the grief is unbelievable, but it must be even worse when your daughter's been killed like that. Someone must know something."

"Well, there's one person out there who definitely knows something. Say, do you have anything going on, later?"

A couple of hours later, the working day was in full swing. After the morning news conference, Gillian and a number of other reporters had gone out on stories, but Cooper was currently writing short articles from a particularly unremarkable set of press releases.

His mobile phone surprised him when it burst into life in his pocket, causing him to jump a little in his seat.

Cooper fumbled to dig it out and peered at the display. It was Sullivan's home number, he was certain of it.

He answered and pressed the phone to his ear.

"Hello?"

"Hello."

A voice this time, a male voice, but definitely not Sullivan. It had a slightly high-pitched, soft delivery. Cooper blinked, confused.

"Er, who's calling please?"

"You're Tim Cooper."

"Yes."

"I found your card here. Thought I'd give you a call. Again."

"*You* called last night?"

"Yes."

Cooper frowned. His heart fluttered against his ribcage.

"So…who are you, and what're you calling about?"

"Well, seeing as I found a reporter's card here, I thought I'd give you the scoop. They're dead. All of them."

"What?"

The inside of Cooper's mouth felt dry. His heart sped up. He felt a horrible, sudden wave of panic, the kind that crept over him when he realized he'd lost or forgotten something important, but worse.

"Is this a joke?"

"No joke. They're dead. I killed them."

"Who's dead?"

One or two of his nearby colleagues exchanged anxious glances.

"The guy and the two kids. Just thought you should know. I don't care how old the kids are, you know. The bodies are still warm when I'm inside them. They don't talk back. They don't issue commands. You should try it sometime."

Cooper couldn't breathe. "No. You didn't..."

"And, um, I was just wondering what you thought of that reporter. What's her name? Ah, yes...Gillian? She's quite...fetching, isn't she? She was here not too long ago. Maybe I'll pay here a visit."

The caller hung up.

Cooper sat still in his chair, stunned, the phone seemingly stuck to the side of his head. He didn't know what to think.

"Tim, are you okay? What's happened?"

It was Janet, the education reporter. He turned to face her and saw several other concerned faces beside hers.

"I don't know if someone's pissing about, or what, but I think we might have to call the police."

And he had to call Gillian.

As the caller had so earnestly insisted, it was not a joke. Sullivan and his children were dead. His nine-year-old son had been beaten to death and dragged into the bathroom. The fourteen-year daughter had been cut to ribbons and then raped, just like the Burrows girl. Sullivan had been completely eviscerated, the intestines removed and subsequently dropped into a pile beside the corpse.

Gillian wasn't picking up her phone, or answering text messages. Cooper was supposed to meet up with her at a bar near the newspaper's building. He was embroiled in the Sullivan murders—while he worried about his coworker's life, he was a witness to the gruesome triple-murder that took place in Halton, a block away from the Burrows murder.

A boy. A father. A daughter shredded and thereafter raped.

When Cooper was questioned by the police, they showed him pictures from the crime scene. The boy was beaten so badly that his likeness wasn't identifiable. Cooper's stomach wouldn't allow him to look at the other pictures. He tried to explain that they needed to find Gillian, that her life depended on it...

The grisly murders made the national news. TV, radio, and print from around the country descended on the area to report on what appeared to be a pulse-heightening serial killer case. It was certainly the biggest story to hit the city in a long while. Each new development made the front page, but a fortnight after the triple murder, no one had been arrested. Door to door calls were made in the area where it happened, and every possible line of inquiry was explored. How could no one have seen anything? Heard anything? People didn't just walk in and out of houses and cut people up without being noticed. It simply wasn't possible.

And Gillian simply disappeared.

Meanwhile, the familiar pattern of tragedy, tributes, and appeals played out. Teachers sang the praises of the young kids. Sullivan's sister and friends talked of his friendliness and reliability, of how good a father he'd been. His sister led the fruitless calls for information. Her grief was broadcast to the nation so that people could transmit their sympathy and personally thank God that their family had not been destroyed in such a way.

And Gillian. Gone.

In the throes of nightmare, Cooper would thrash within his sheets every night. Gillian. Their last conversation repeated itself over and over again within his fragmented semi-consciousness. He wanted to tell her about Halton, about the recent murders. He wanted to tell her about the phone call.

Maybe he could have saved her life. The Sullivans were already dead when the killer placed the call, weren't they? Shouldn't he have looked for Gillian instead of going to the police about a family that was already butchered?

When the police questioned him about Gillian, there was nothing to say.

Four days after the 'Sullivan Massacre,' two garbage handlers discovered Gillian's corpse in the dumpster behind the bar where her and Cooper were supposed to meet. She'd been gutted and violated like the other horrendous murders. A macabre collection of flies and maggots had gorged themselves upon her exposed innards.

The story made the front page.

How did the killer know where she was going to be? The police were unable to turn up any clues.

The press machine can be a valuable tool in the process of justice. Campaigns and investigations can raise awareness, block travesties, and reveal uneasy truths. Police appeals, whether delivered to the public by the written word or the spoken, can lead to the eventual capture and incarceration of dangerous individuals.

Cases like this put the fear of God into people. The victims weren't slain in dark alleyways or deserted parks. Any world where someone could step uninvited into your home, and rip you asunder, was not a happy one.

He made a special effort to double check that the doors were locked at night. His parents, and certain friends, offered to put him up in their homes. His mom and dad were actually quite insistent he return home when they learned exactly what happened, but he stubbornly refused all offers.

Most people were understandably curious, almost excited, when they found out about the call; that he'd actually talked to the killer. What did he sound like? Did he sound weird, or demented? Was he charming, like Hannibal Lecter?

What could he tell them? What did he tell the police? It was an unremarkable voice, calm, collected, and devoid of a distinguishable accent. The detectives had not liked that. They thought they were looking for a local man and would have loved him to confirm that.

He constantly thought about that voice. He imagined who it belonged to, the face and the hair, the clothes and the body.

He contemplated a back story, an occupation, and a home, but he didn't dare give his creation a name.

It was the day before Cooper was due back at work, and he was looking forward to it. It would give him some focus, some drive.

They'd keep him well away from anything heavy for a little while. He'd probably get some nice, cushy assignment to begin with, and that would suit him just fine.

The morning was spent tidying the house and doing a little shopping. He met a friend for a pint in the afternoon and they talked about everyday things: the weather, football, the red-headed beauty behind the bar.

In the evening, he and his housemate shared a pizza, cracked open a pair of lagers, and settled down to watch some TV. A soap opera full of screaming, sobbing, dysfunctional families. A comedy about a hapless father.

At about eleven, Cooper called it a night; he was determined to be in decent condition for work the next day. He headed upstairs and left his comrade in front of the box, watching some late night discussion program with vague interest.

He readied his outfit for the morning, washed, brushed his teeth, and then crawled into bed, pulling the duvet up to his hair and burying himself in its embrace. He was tired and the lager played its part as well; he was fast asleep within minutes.

He groggily awoke sometime later with a slight hangover. He rubbed his eyes and glanced at the bedside clock with its digits glowing red in the gloom: it was two in the morning.

With a long groan, he rolled over onto his back and shut his eyes. All he'd wanted was a good night's sleep, but his housemate must have woken him when he'd finally seen fit to turn in.

Cooper cursed the man silently, but then he heard the distant murmur of voices drifting up from the television below. He had to still be downstairs, unless he'd forgotten to turn the thing off. He opened his eyes again and yawned.

Maybe he was just nervous about going back to work. He'd had disruptive nights in the past when exams had been looming or he'd had some other big event the next day. For the first few days after the Sullivan family's massacre, he'd had a bad time trying to sleep properly, but he overcame that.

Gillian. When he closed his eyes, her warm smile haunted him anew. She wouldn't be there, tomorrow.

Sleep wasn't going to return. Not now.

In his bedroom's gloom, there were murky shapes where his desk and cupboards should be; the clothes on his chair formed the outline of a grossly malformed human being.

But there was some faint illumination after all.

He thought he'd shut his bedroom door, as he always did, but there it was, open and gaping. A long, broad panel of pale moonlight shone through the space between the frames. Then, a second later, the light was blocked out by the tall silhouette of a lean figure.

Cooper blinked. His heart raced. His thoughts were scattered, feverish.

He was not imagining things. There was a man-shaped shadow there, just feet away, and he was certain it wasn't his housemate.

He sat up and opened his mouth to say something. His breathing was ragged and fast.

The stranger's face still eluded him. He went to switch on his bedside lamp as if the light would somehow banish the demon as it had when he was a child. He wasn't quite frozen with fear. Not yet.

"Hello again," the figure said.

The soft, calm voice was unmistakably familiar. Cooper felt his chest tighten and his bladder threatened to fail; the panic really hit home.

There was a cricket bat he'd placed near the bed, more for peace of mind than anything else, but now he really *was* too scared to move, to reach for it. This new-found paralysis almost gave him hope. Could it be a nightmare after all?

He struggled for words. Nothing, no insult or plea, seemed quite adequate.

"Why me?" he blurted out finally, quailing amongst the covers.

The figure said nothing but advanced, striding forward purposefully. Cooper finally got a look at his tormentor. The moonlight's glow formed a halo around the dome-shaped head. The man flexed and crinkled fingers with the plastic gloves over them.

"Bob," Cooper managed a faint gasp through his teeth.

"You did such a great job on your Sullivan interview," Bob nodded. "But sometimes, you understand, I get so...carried away. I've read so many stories. I've seen so many pictures. I've done the death knocks. There were so many evenings where sleep eluded me as I couldn't help but hear the words of grief and horror."

"Gillian..."

"Beautiful girl. She looked so much like my ex-wife. I never wanted kids, you see. I couldn't handle being around so much beauty, so much innocence. I overheard your conversation with poor Gilliam, and when she recognized me at the bar, everything else was easy. One thing you must know is that a good reporter *makes* the news. I'm simply giving the people what they want. In return, I get what I want."

Cooper's fear held him hostage as Bob enclosed his hands around his throat. He struggled as best he could, fighting wildly, but it was a hopeless contest. Ridiculous sounds gurgled from his mouth as his eyes bulged. Bright dots flashed within his vision.

Bob removed one hand and quickly brandished a blade; light glinted off the edge of the weapon's long, jagged edge.

"The headline is going to read, 'Night Stalker Kills Again.' I get to name myself. Isn't that wonderful?"

Despite it all—through the pain, the terror, and an overwhelming sense of despair—he couldn't help but wonder, with a reporter's curiosity, whether his death would make the front pages.

UNDER SIEGE

DAVID H. DONAGHE

I was down in the garden, leaning on my hoe one cool evening around sunset, and I was watching Roxy, while she bent over to pull some weeds. She had on those damned, Daisy Dukes that drive me nuts, with the cheeks of her ass hanging out of the bottom of her shorts. Her copious breasts strained the fabric of her wife beater t-shirt, and her hard nipples pushed up the cotton material.

Thank God for the cold night air, I thought and then grinned. I stepped to the side to catch the view down the deep valley of cleavage between her breasts. A silly grin crossed her face; she stood up, arching her back and stretched, which caused her massive mammary glands to jut forward. She leaned back, cupped both of her breasts in her hands and gave them a shake for my benefit. "Mike, you're such a male chauvinist pig," she said, laughing.

For a few seconds, I found it hard to breathe and my heart did a drum roll. I felt something rising in my lower regions. "Yeah, but you love me anyway, dear," I said, and that was when the attack occurred. My name is Mike Monroe, former owner of Monroe's Paranormal Investigations, and Roxy—her real name is Roxanne Delaney—is my partner. When the swine flu gave the world a sucker punch and the United States Government collapsed, Roxy and I escaped, leaving the big city behind and found a safe haven in a survival camp in the high desert of Southern California. Everyone here calls this place the bunker. Years ago, some wealthy businessmen bought a chunk of property in the desert that had once been a former military installation. It held several cement pillboxes above-ground with a massive subterranean complex underneath. The owner broadcasted a rightwing radio show before the collapse, and when the world took a powder, he invited people here. They have one rule: you don't work, you don't eat.

We barely escaped from the city with our lives, and we hooked up with a motorcycle club known as The Road Dogs along the way. Most days I ride with the club going on scavenger runs looking for supplies while Roxy works in the medical center, but today I decided to help with the gardening—gardening brings me peace. The alarm sounded as gunfire erupted from the perimeter. I looked up, the smell of gunpowder filling the air. A horde of flesh-eating zombies were storming the perimeter in mass. Here at the bunker, we have razor wire ringing the compound, plus a series of trenches and fighting positions fifty yards in, but still five-hundred yards away from the main compound.

"Oh shit!" Roxy yelled. Her face turned pale and she reached over and grabbed her Ruger Mini- 14 where it was lying on her jacket on the ground.

"Tell me about it," I said, grabbing my AR-15 from beside me. "I thought we got rid of this problem when the world took a shit." I should have known better, especially after that time when I was with The Road Dogs and those zombie sons of bitches caught us in the old Harvey House in Barstow. At the time, I thought it was just an isolated incident, but that's another story.

Roxy ran for the perimeter, I chased after her, not failing to notice the swish of her backside and the sway of her large breasts under her shirt. People screamed, running for their fighting positions, the sound of gunfire echoing across the desert. The sound of the zombies grunting filled the air. Roxy and I dived into a fighting position. I slapped a clip into the AR and we opened up on the mangy flesh-eaters by the road. I froze for a moment.

How can there be so many of them? I wondered. There were literally thousands of the smelly, decaying bastards climbing up the fence. I opened up on the fence-line, riddling the undead corpses with bullets, but still they came.

"Shit," Roxy said, kneeling down and grabbing her knee. "I scraped my knee." Blood oozed from her knee and dripped down her sexy leg.

"I think we've got a little bit more to worry about right now than those sexy knees," I said and opened up with my AR. I emptied a clip and slapped in another.

The guys on the perimeter peppered the zombies on the fence with small arms fire. The razor wire caught some of the smelly vermin, but their mates just crawled over them. Dark blood and using puss flowed down their putrid bodies to the ground. The ones that made it over the fence dropped to the ground and charged our position. The thunderous roar of gunfire and the acidic smell of gunpowder suffused the air, but then the wind changed and the putrid smell of the undead flesh drifted our way.

"God, that's enough to gag a fucking maggot," I said.

"Tell me about it. That smells worse than rotten pussy," Roxy quipped and emptied a clip at the flesh-eaters. I usually enjoyed watching her breasts bounce back and forth when she fired a rifle, but I barely had time to notice.

I laughed. "Have I ever mentioned that you have a vulgar mouth on you? Such language. What would your mother say if she heard you right now?"

"Oh, blow it out your backside, Mike," she said and opened up on the approaching zombie horde.

"Head shots! Remember, head shots, people!" I yelled to the other defenders manning the perimeter. We mowed them down, but still they came, like the legions of the damned. Several jumped into our trench. A small female zombie with rotten teeth and sagging flesh ripped the throat out of a young man standing next to me. He screamed and fell back with blood spewing from his throat. I butt-stroked the smelly bitch with my AR as three more jumped on my back. Roxy pulled two of them off me and I flipped the other one over my shoulder. He tried to get up, but I smashed him in the head with the butt of my rifle.

"The claymores! Blow the claymores people!" I yelled, realizing that we were about to be over run. Then someone threw the switch, blowing the claymores. There was a loud explosion that took my breath away. It knocked me on my ass and the gaggle of zombies on the perimeter ceased to exist. Dust and debris filled the air. When the dust cleared, there was nothing there but something that looked like rancid hamburger meat, but still they came.

"To the bunker!" I yelled. "Fall back to the bunker!"

We retreated, heading to the bunker while the men manning fifty caliber machine guns gave us covering fire from the top of the main pillbox: a round reinforced cement bunker housing the office complex and the communications center. I looked over my shoulder and saw a zombie take a woman down. The stinky bastard ripped open the poor woman's stomach, then pulled a long coil of intestine from her body and started chewing on one end. Blood and gore dripped down the zombie's arm while it enjoyed the snack. I whirled around and put a double tap through its brainpan. Several squads covered our rear while we climbed up the ladders. Although my heart hammered inside my chest and I felt like I was going to shit myself because of the zombies nipping at my heels, I admired the view of Roxy's shapely ass while she climbed up.

She glanced down and caught me looking. "Mike, this is hardly the time," she said, but I just shrugged, a shit-eating grin crossing my face. I followed her up the ladder. Once everyone was up top, we pulled up the ladders and I looked down at the swarm of zombies below.

"We're fucked," I said and we headed down into the bunker. The men manning the fifties continued firing, mowing down the flesh-eaters.

When I climbed down the ladder into the Command Center, the CO yelled, "Monroe! Get your ass over here!" People ran back and forth, securing the compound. I hustled over to where he sat at a computer console, monitoring the surveillance system. The rest of the survivors from outside stood around in the Command Center, letting the adrenaline rush subside. I looked down at the screen, seeing the video feed from outside and I felt like I was going to shit my drawers. Roxy stepped up next to me and I felt a slight pressure of her left breast against my right arm. Bodies of the zombies, now dead for good, began to pile up on the ground in front of the pillbox.

"What is this shit? I thought that when the swine flu hit we were done with this kind of thing!" Colonel Roberts said.

"Me too, boss, but I guess with all the bodies lying around after they died off, the virus spread," I said.

The colonel rubbed his grizzled chin. "I read your file, Monroe. What are we supposed to do about this?"

I remained silent for a few seconds, studying the computer monitor. "Once that pile of bodies gets high enough, the rest will be able to climb up on top of the pillbox. We'll need to pull the guys on the fifties inside before that happens."

The colonel nodded. "Right. We can stay in here under siege for a couple of months easy, but that's not the way I operate. Like I said, I read your file, Monroe. You have experience with this kind of thing. Do you have any ideas?" The colonel swiveled in his chair to face me.

A devious grin crossed my face. "Well, Colonel Roberts, sir, I do. It's gonna get dark soon. Let's pull the men on top inside and button this place down. We still have a few tanker trucks in the motor pool, don't we?"

"Yes we do. They're full of gas. What's your plan?"

I chuckled. "Tomorrow, at day break, I'll take one of the tankers outside and turn on the valve under the tank. I'll make a few runs around the complex, pouring gas everywhere. Once we empty the tanker, we'll bring it back inside and then send some boys up top with flamethrowers. We'll burn the SOBs alive. We'll have ourselves a zombie barbeque. I'll need a driver, though."

"I can handle that," Roxy said.

Colonel Roberts ran his hand through his short gray hair. "Okay. I know you two are a team, but be careful, Miss Delaney. The men would put me in front of a firing squad if we lost you."

Roxy blushed.

I laughed. "They do love their eye candy."

Colonel Roberts stood up. "Let's go people! Let's get those men off the roof and seal this place up tight. I want every door locked down and every hatch buttoned up!"

The people inside the Command Center dispersed, going about their business. The men on the roof fired several more rounds at the host of undead flesh-eaters on the ground, then climbed down the ladder, after securing the hatch to the roof.

"I don't feel so good," Roxy said, fanning the air in front of her face. Dried blood covered her knee, but the wound had already stopped bleeding.

"It's not that time of the month yet, is it?" I asked and put my arm around her.

"No. I feel faint," she said and fell against me.

I put my arms around her to keep her from falling. "Let's get you down to our quarters. You need to take your medicine," I said and led her away.

After leading Roxy through a warren of dimly-lit, underground passageways, we stepped into our little room in the housing area. Roxy lay down on our small bed and pulled an Army blanket over her body. She had the chills one minute and then seemed about to burn up the next. Sweat beaded-up on her forehead and for a few minutes, she seemed delirious. I took a camp stove from under the bed, fired it up, and poured some water into a pot. I put the pot of water on to boil and then took a ziplock bag from the top drawer of Roxy's dresser and put some leaves from a plant into the pot of water.

"Mike...it's too early. The moon won't be full for another week."

"I know, darling, but it looks like your time of the month is coming early, now be a good little wolfgirl and drink your wolf bane." About a year ago, we went down to a little town on the Mexican border on a case, and a werewolf attacked Roxy and bit her. "You might want to get undressed if you don't want to ruin your clothes when you change," I said.

"You just want to see me naked. I'm probably just coming down with the flu. I mean the regular one, not the swine flu. But you're right, I think I'll get undressed and take a little nap. I'll feel better when I wake up. Turn around," she said, rising to her feet.

I chuckled, taking her arm to steady her. "What's gotten into you? Since when did you get modest?" I turned around, but another shit-eating grin crossed my face when I glanced in the mirror hanging on the wall to my left and saw Roxy's reflection in all her glory when she stripped off her clothes.

She climbed into bed and pulled the covers up to her neck. "You can turn around now."

I turned around and poured the concoction in the pot into a coffee cup. "Here, take your medicine," I said, holding my nose.

"I don't want to. That stuff tastes terrible," she said, but then leaned forward when I handed her the cup. The blanket fell away, revealing her lovely breasts. A grin crossed her face as she pulled the blanket back up and said, "Okay, you can put your eyes back in your head now." She took the cup, had a drink, made a sour face, and said, "Damn, that stuff tastes horrible."

"But you know it's good for you," I said. Leaning forward, I kissed her and at the same time I snapped a manacle around her wrist, chaining her to the bed. Roxy's eyes widened in anger, but I grabbed the other maniacal by the head of the bed, snapped it on her other wrist, then moved down to the foot of the bed. Before she knew what was happening, I had her legs chained to the bed as well.

"Mike, this isn't necessary! It's just the flu!" she yelled, struggling against the chains.

"You know I can't take that chance, baby doll," I said. When we'd first moved in, I'd secured the chains to the cement floor under the bed, sealing them with cement.

"Mike Monroe, you no good son-of-a-bitch! Take these chains off me right now, damn you!"

"Sorry, but why don't you just be a good little wolfgirl and go to sleep. It'll all be over in the morning. I'm gonna go over to the lounge and have a beer with the fellas." I let out a chuckle as I stepped out of the room and the sound of Roxy screaming obscenities at me echoed down the hallway.

A few minutes later, I found a seat in a blue lazy boy in the lounge, and popped the top on a beer. Colonel Roberts came in and sat down in a chair next to me. We called him the colonel, but he wasn't former military; he just ran the organization in a military fashion.

"Damn, I couldn't believe it when I looked at the monitor and saw those sons of bitches. Zombies. It's hard to believe," the colonel said.

I handed him a beer from the cooler sitting next to my chair and said, "Not for me. With all those dead bodies all over the place who knows what diseases are out there."

The colonel nodded. He picked up the remote for the TV and pointed it at the screen mounted high on the wall. He changed the station and the video feed from outside filled the screen.

"Look at those things. They're all over the damned place," he said. "What do we do if we can't kill them all? We can't stay here underground and under siege indefinitely."

I heaved a sigh. "We'll get them, sir, but while we're here enjoying our little survivor's haven, the world's going to Hell. If you only knew the things I've seen."

"It might not be as bad as you think. There are others."

"Others?"

"Other survival compounds scattered across the country," he said. "I've talked to some of them on the shortwave. There's talk of forming some loose type of federation."

"That wouldn't be a bad thing, as long as we didn't go back to the old system. It was beyond fixing."

"You're preaching to the choir, son," the colonel said and took a sip of his beer.

"Has anyone heard from The Road Dogs?" I asked.

The colonel shook his head. "No, but with all that undead scum outside, they're probably hiding out in the hills somewhere."

"I hope they're all right. I should have been out there with them."

"I know you're worried, but it's lucky for us you were here."

"Oh yeah, lucky me," I said.

"I mean it, Monroe. We need you. You're the only one who has had experience with those damned things. I don't know what we'd do without you."

"You've got some good men here, Colonel. You'd make out all right without me."

"Maybe, but I'm still glad you're here. I'm glad Miss Delaney's here, too. The men love her. She's good for morale."

I laughed. "She's entertaining, but some of the women don't like her."

"They're just jealous."

While outside, the zombies stumbled around, looking for a way to get inside the bunker, the colonel and I continued to talk and drink for the next couple of hours. Then someone was shaking my arm. It startled me and I looked up into the face of a young, dark-headed woman. "I think you better go check on your woman," she said. "She's making a hell of a racket down there in your room. You can hear her howling all the way down the hall."

I nodded to her. "You know how she gets, the closer we get to the full moon and all, but I'll go check on her." I stood up. "It's been good talking to you, sir," I said to the colonel and left. I ambled through a maze of passageways until I reached the living area and then headed down the main corridor to our room.

"Mike! Thank God, you're back! Turn me loose!" Roxy yelled when I entered the room. She thrashed about and must have tossed off her blankets while I was gone because she was laying there totally naked, struggling against the chains. Her large breasts jiggled back and forth as she struggled to free herself. Enjoying the show, I took in her beautiful body in a glance, watching her breasts bounce back and forth. My eyes drifted south, taking in her long sexy legs and the tiny patch of hair between her legs.

"Nice trim," I said.

"Shut up, Mike! Let me go!"

"Sorry, baby doll, no can do."

"You don't understand! They're coming!"

"Settle down. Who's coming?" I asked and took a seat across from her.

She shook her head. "I don't know! Something…someone. A pack I think!"

That got my attention. "What do you mean a pack?" I took a cigar out of my shirt pocket.

"People like me, but more powerful! Werewolves! I think that's why the change is coming early!" she screamed, still struggling with her chains.

My eyes widened. "Werewolves? Coming here? How do you know?"

"I had a vision!"

I took a Zippo lighter from my pants pocket and fired up my cigar. A cloud of tobacco smoke filled the air. "A vision? What type of vision?"

"I don't know. I can't explain it. You know that when my time gets close, my senses become hyper sensitive!"

"Okay. How many and when will they get here?" I asked, taking a toke on my cigar.

She calmed down, quit struggling against the chains, and said, "I don't know, but they're close. I think it's a big pack."

I nodded and stood up. "Right now we've got this zombie problem outside. We'll deal with them tomorrow. You get some rest. I'll unlock your chains in the morning."

"Unlock them now! Turn me loose, damn you!" she screamed.

I shook my head. "Sorry. I can't do that. If you'd learn some control, those chains wouldn't be necessary."

She threw herself against the chains, screaming in rage and the change came over her. Her body sprouted long course hair, her legs and arms morphed and her back arched as she changed into a wolf. She let out a blood-curdling roar and slashed at me with her claws.

"I think I'll find other sleeping arrangements for the night, wolfgirl," I said. I stepped out the door and walked down the hallway. Shaking my head, I let out a chuckle, listing to her enraged howl echo down the corridor.

At five a.m. the following morning, I strolled down to our room and entered it. I had two cups of coffee in my hands. Roxy lay on her stomach with her derriere pointed at the sky, fast asleep.

"Up and at it, darlin'. How are you feelin' this morning?" I asked while turning on the light.

Roxy groaned, rolled onto her side, and put her feet on the floor. "Like a warm bag of shit, no thanks to you. Do you know how hard it is to sleep when someone chains you to a bed? God, it's cold in here," she said, holding her hand up to shield her eyes from the light.

I handed her a cup of coffee and then began to unlock her chains. "Sorry about that, but get dressed. We have some zombies to kill." I waited while Roxy dressed; we finished our coffee, gathered our gear, and passed through the maze of underground passageways to the motor pool. Colonel Roberts and a squad of troops were waiting for us. They had a tanker truck parked a few yards from the massive roll-up door that led to the outside.

"Are you ready for this, Monroe?" Colonel Roberts asked.

I shrugged. "As ready as I'll ever be. You guys watch out. As soon as we open that door, those damned zombies are gonna storm the place. Wait until we have the truck started and pulled up next to the door before you open it." I nodded at Roxy and said, "You drive, babe."

Roxy climbed up on the running board of the truck with her Ruger Mini-14 strapped over her back. I stood on the ground for a few seconds, admiring her shapely ass, which hung out of her Daisy Duke shorts, then walked around to the passenger side of the truck. I climbed onto the running board, tossed my AR-15 into the cab, and climbed inside.

The colonel nodded up at Roxy and said, "You be careful, little lady."

Roxy gave him a smile. "Sure thing, Colonel." She started the truck, the rumble of the engine reverberating through the motor pool and the smell of diesel exhaust filling the air.

I glanced over at Roxy. "As soon as we pull outside, I want you to stop the truck. I'm gonna jump out, run around to your side, and open the valve underneath the tank. I'll need you to cover me with your Mini-14."

Roxy's face looked pale and her hands trembled. "What about the zombies? There's too many of them."

I nodded. "Hopefully, I'll be able to open the valve and get back in the truck before they mob me."

Colonel Roberts opened the door, letting in the cool morning breeze as a mob of zombies tried to pour inside, but the troops in the motor pool opened up on them with automatic weapons. Roxy pulled through the door, running over several flesh-eaters. She drove toward a clear spot ten yards away. She slammed on the brakes, causing me to fly forward, put the truck in park, and said, "Make it quick!"

I jumped out of the cab and fell flat on my face. Leaping to my feet, I ran into three decayed, maggot-infested zombies. One tried to lunge for my throat, but I butt-stroked him with my AR and shot the other two, putting three rounds each in what was left of their brainpans. I noticed several more heading my way. One had been a woman. Her shirt was in tatters, revealing her sagging and decayed flesh. I noticed a maggot worming its way from underneath the skin of her left cheek. She held her arms out in front of her and let out a groan, her odor wafting on the wind. I dived under the truck and struggled with the valve, trying to let the gasoline out. What looked like fifty or more of the undead stumbled my way.

"Hurry up Mike!" Roxy yelled and opened up with her Mini-14 from the cab of the truck. The sound of gunfire filled the air and hot brass rained down from Roxy's window.

Finally, I managed to open the valve and gasoline gushed onto the ground. Gasoline fumes caused my eyes to water. I ran back around to the passenger side and right into a wall of undead bodies. Swinging my AR like a club, I managed to knock several of them to the ground. Jumping over their bodies, I climbed into the cab of the truck.

"Now what, Mike?" Roxy asked.

"Go! Go! Go! Mow them down!" I yelled. She ran over ten of the fragrant bastards that were in front of the truck, splattering their filthy undead bodies all over the grille. We began to circle the compound, emptying the gasoline everywhere. Guts, heads, torsos, legs and arms, along with several whole bodies, flew into the air as the grille smashed into the evil vermin. Dark, syrupy blood and guts covered the windshield. Roxy turned on the windshield wipers, but that just spread blood and gore all over the glass.

"Oh shit, Mike! I can hardly see!" she yelled.

"Keep driving goddamn it! Mow 'em down!"

We circled the compound several times, but they still converged on the truck. One ugly-looking zombie with half of his head blown away climbed up onto the running board on my side and tried to climb in my window.

"I don't think so, Stinky," I said and slammed my elbow into what remained of its face. The body flew backward, fell to the ground and the truck's rear wheels ran over its head. Looking in the sideview mirror, I watched the head pop like a ripe melon.

When the tank ran dry, I radioed in to the Command Center, using a hand-held radio, and they opened the door to the motor pool. When Roxy pulled into the motor pool, a squad waiting inside clubbed down the zombies hanging on to the side of the truck and took them out with well-placed head shots. The doors to the motor pool were barely closed when another squad climbed out of the main hatch and on the roof and opened up on the zombies below with flamethrowers. A ragging inferno erupted, and the men up top turned off their flamethrowers and climbed back inside the bunker, sealing the hatch once more. The stench of rotten and burning flesh seeped in through the air filtration system. After parking the truck, Roxy and I joined the colonel in the Command Center. He turned on the surveillance system and we monitored the carnage outside on the monitor. All I could see was a wall of flames. "Talk about your barbeques, but I don't think I want anything to do with that rotten meat," I said, laughing.

"What? You don't like barbequed zombie?" Roxy asked.

"I think they'll be a little over-done by the time that fire goes out. This might take a while. Let's go have a beer," Colonel Roberts said.

The fire raged for several more hours. Roxy and I were lounging in our room when a knock came on the door.

"Who is it?" I asked.

"This is Corporal Johnson. The CO wants you in the Command Center. He says you're gonna want to see this."

Roxy and I headed up to the Command Center with Johnson and joined the colonel. We found a couple of empty chairs and sat next to him, viewing the scene outside through the computer monitor. Charred corpses littered the ground and black smoke filled the air, but through the smoke we saw what looked like thousands of flesh-eaters coming from the road to join the party.

"God, how can there be so many of them?" Colonel Roberts asked in frustration.

I paused, shaking off the despair and shook my head. "I don't know."

"Look, out by the road," Roxy said pointing to the monitor.

We saw what looked like hundreds of vehicles pulling up out front by the razor wire. People climbed out, looking wild and wooly, and converged on the compound. As if on command, the new group morphed, changing into werewolves to then launch an attack on the flesh-eating zombies. I saw zombie heads, along with an assortment of other body parts, flying through the air as the werewolves ripped the bodies asunder.

"How can they change like that on command? It's daylight and the full moon's not for another day or two," Roxy asked.

"These old boys ain't like you. They weren't bitten. They were born this way," I replied.

"What do we do now?" Colonel Roberts asked.

"You know all those silver coins you have stored down in the vault?" I said.

"Yeah, so?" the colonel replied.

"Let's go get 'em. We need to start making bullets," I said, then leaned back to take in the scene on the monitor. The sun set over the Mojave while I watched in amazement as the battle between the werewolves and zombies raged on.

Want more of Roxy and Mike? Then check out the novel:
Monroe's Paranormal Investigations
published by Living Dead Press

THE BUS

WAYNE C. ROGERS

Danny Stiles was one pissed off man.

He stared at the Double-Double Bonus Video Poker machine in disbelief and felt the blood rushing through him as a deep, boiling rage threatened to overtake him. Stiles had lost his entire paycheck in less than four hours—nearly eight hundred dollars—and he hadn't even hit one four-of-a-kind.

Not one!

The rent was due on his apartment in two days, along with his electric and telephone bills. He now had no money to pay them.

Forget food.

His sorry ass was stone broke, except for the two singles stuck inside his right boot that were supposed to be used for bus fare.

"Here's your drink, sir," a shapely blonde-haired cocktail waitress said. She was dressed in a blue bustier, dark blue briefs, and black pantyhose. "You ordered a Heineken."

"That was twenty minutes ago!" Stiles shouted.

"I'm sorry, but it's a Friday night and we're short-handed."

"I don't care what day it is or how many people are working! This place is a shit hole!"

"Sir, if you keep using vulgar language, I'm going to have to call security."

"Do I look like I care, lady?" Stiles took the green bottle of beer off her round tray, chugged half of it in one deep swallow, and threw the bottle at the poker machine's screen. The monitor exploded in a shower of broken glass; sparks flew everywhere from the electrical wiring as the beer soaked the game machine's guts.

"That's it, I'm calling security!" the frightened waitress shrieked.

"And after you do that, you can kiss my royal ass," Stiles said. He noticed the other patrons staring in his direction. "What're you looking at? Mind your own business."

The cocktail waitress, however, didn't have to call the Blue Bayou Casino security. Two men in black suits were already approaching Stiles with their hands resting on tasers. Stiles had had several beers during the course of the night, but he wasn't drunk—he could still react to a given situation with a bit of clarity. He picked up the stool he'd been sitting on and whipped it around into the first security officer, knocking him to the carpet. As the second man attempted to pull his weapon, Stiles rushed into him and delivered two fast blows with his fists—one to the stomach and one to the side of the face. When the second officer went down, Stiles turned to his audience and bowed.

"Now, all of you can go to hell in a bread basket," he announced.

"You'll be there long before us," an elderly man declared while turning back to his machine.

"I wish," Stiles replied. "Hell has to be better than this damn city."

When he realized that four more security guards were running toward him, Stiles decided it was time to leave. He didn't want to spend the night in jail for assault and battery in addition to destruction of property. He moved through the gathering crowd of onlookers, passed the colorful gambling machines, and made his way through the front exits that faced West Tropicana Avenue.

Stiles rushed through the parking lot, trying not to draw attention. He walked up a small, grassy embankment and darted across Tropicana without looking, hoping to get across the wide street and to the bus stop before he was caught. Early evening had settled over the sprawling metropolis of sin and depravity; the thick crowd along the boulevard could provide an ample cover for Stiles to make his escape.

Stiles breathed a sigh of relief as he made his way across the street—he was going to make it. A silver Honda Accord pulled out in front of the Blue Bayou's property.

The driver never saw Stiles.

The corner of the car's front bumper clipped the angry drunk, spinning him around and knocking him hard to the pavement. Stiles landed several feet away in the center lane and nearly got hit a second time by a Ford pickup. The driver of the Ford slammed on the brakes and skidded around Stiles like a stunt driver in a Hollywood movie; the tires smoked and the brakes screamed.

Stiles couldn't move for a full minute. His entire body ached, and he didn't know if anything, or everything, was broken. The pain was mind-numbing. The street was eerily silent after that chaotic, near-death experience.

"Ah, Jesus," he groaned and opened his left eye.

It took some effort, but the degenerate gambler managed to rise to his knees— he agonizingly rose to his feet, and the sharp pain that raced through his injured body nearly forced him to cry out. He looked around and saw the Honda's driver standing in front of the car's headlights, staring at him. The pickup truck was thirty feet down the other way, the engine idle. The driver sat behind the wheel for a few seconds, then drove off like a bat out of hell.

Waiting around for the cops to show and give him a two-hundred dollar jaywalking ticket seemed like a bad idea. Stiles limped over to the curb on the opposite side of the street, avoiding the oncoming traffic. He was still cursing under his breath for being such an idiot and losing all of his money in the Bayou. Distant police sirens caused the crowd to pause; the lure of revelry wasn't enough to overcome the innate desire to linger near the scene of an accident. He made his way down to the deserted bus stop. No one followed him.

For once, he was lucky.

The bus showed up just as he reached the small, plexiglass haven where people normally waited for their transportation. He stood amongst the cobwebs and faded, torn movie posters that were plastered against the walls while he watched his ride arrive. The sirens were closer. Stiles watched as curious pedestrians cautiously approached the Honda. Why would anyone care so much about a car crash in which there weren't any fatalities? The guy nearly killed Stiles! It took a shitty driver to drive a shitty car.

The bus engine was a welcome sound; two cop cars had arrived on the scene, and one sat in the middle of the street to block traffic.

Instead of being brown or gray, however, this bus was painted black. Stiles figured it had something to do with another city promotion. The bus system had been running promotions all month to encourage more people to use it. The bus slowly came to a halt, and its accordion doors opened for him. He grabbed the metal handle on the right and pulled himself up the three steps, groaning from the pain in his hip and back.

"The money's in my boot," Stiles announced without glancing at the driver. As he bent over to retrieve the bills, he got a whiff of *something* foul and putrid. It smelled like rotting meat and almost made him gag. "What the…"

He stood up and looked at the bus driver. The guy was staring back at him with a big, stupid-ass grin on his face like he'd just heard the funniest joke in the world. His thick, gray eyebrows squatted over rheumatic eyes. As the lips seemed to curl back painfully into a Cheshire cat display, Stiles couldn't help but stare at the black, tar-rotted teeth. Strands of thin, wiry gray hair hung like tattered threads from an unraveling, mottled scalp.

"What the hell stinks in here?" Stiles wrinkled his nose while holding the money in his hand. The driver simply stared with the terrible grin painted across his face. Stiles shook his head in disgust. "Sorry."

The driver didn't say a word.

"Screw it," Stiles murmured to himself.

As he started to push the first dollar into the bill acceptor, the driver quickly shook his head and placed his hand over it. His fingernails were incredibly long, and his bony knuckles seemed to stretch the flesh as if the man were nothing more than an uncomfortable skeleton clad in the skin of a homeless man.

"What?" Stiles asked. "The ride's free tonight?"

The bus driver nodded, still smiling that wide, black grin.

"Hey, thanks. I appreciate it."

The driver then pointed to the aisle running down the center of the bus, insinuating that Stiles needed to take a seat.

"Yeah, sure," Stiles said, limping down the narrow aisle. "Whatever."

There weren't many people on the bus at this time of night. Stiles counted seven as he worked his way to the rear. There were five men and two women. All the passengers were staring straight ahead as if they wanted to avoid making eye contact with him. They treated him as if he were some ragged vagrant who sought their mercy in the form of spare change.

He took a seat in the back beside a tinted window.

The appearance of additional blue and red flashing lights across the street caught his attention. He glanced out the window to see what was going on. The Honda Accord was still parked on the other side with the driver talking to a Metro police officer. An ambulance had arrived on the scene. Whatever happened to the Honda's driver, the guy deserved it.

"I wonder what's going on," Stiles said as the bus pulled away from the curb.

Glancing around at the other passengers, he realized that their faces were still staring forward. The flashing blue and red lights hadn't interested them; their thoughts were on more important things. Wouldn't these people at least want to gawk, maybe look for a gurney with a fresh corpse being carted into a waiting ambulance? Wasn't that the allure behind every crime or accident? He looked at the lady sitting closest to him and noticed for the first time how pale her face was.

Her eyes seemed completely devoid of life.

Stiles clenched his fists. The revolting smell inside the bus seemed to seep out of the leather seats. The inside of the bus was incredibly dark; the flashing police lights illuminated the expressionless, stone-faced gazes upon the face of each passenger.

None of the passengers were blinking.

He felt incredibly alone. Nothing seemed right: the bus driver, the passengers—what the hell was going on?

Deciding he needed to get off the bus, Stiles jerked on the cord above his head to let the driver know he wanted the next stop.

No bell rang.

The intercom system didn't turn on to indicate that a stop was requested.

Stiles watched through the window on the right side as the next stop was passed. The following stop was also passed. Unsure what else to do, he got up from his seat and hobbled down the aisle to the front.

"I need to get off," he said to the driver. "I drank too much and feel sick to my stomach."

The driver ignored him, his bony fingers wrapped tightly around the large steering wheel. The same half-crazed grin scarred his face.

"Do you want me to puke all over your bus?" Stiles raised his voice. "I need to get off right now!"

Shifting his attention from the street, the driver's smile slipped into something slightly more grotesque and hideous as he spoke through rotted teeth. "No more stops until we reach our final destination."

"I said you gotta stop this fucking bus!"

The driver simply ignored him.

"I'm going to puke all over you."

"Do what you must, Mr. Stiles," the driver said.

"How do *you* know my name?"

"Why, you're on the passenger's list. I'm *supposed* to pick you up tonight." The bus driver made a *tsk-tsk* sound of annoyance and motioned for Stiles to return to his seat. "All the passengers are to be seated."

"Where's our final destination?" Stiles asked warily and squared his shoulders. He thought he could feel a million eyes upon him while his confrontation with the driver dragged on.

The driver nonchalantly pointed his right forefinger upward to the LED display board above the windshield and rearview mirror that was used to check on the passengers.

Stiles's eyes followed the pointed finger to the board and watched the final destination scroll across, repeating itself over and over again. He opened his mouth to say something, but then shifted his eyes to the rearview mirror and looked at the reflection of his face. One side of his head was caved in. Blood covered both his scalp and face. Glancing back at the digital board, he digested the repeated, glowing words.

Destination Hell... Destination Hell... Destination Hell... Destination Hell...

The words began to blur together.

Glancing back at the passengers, Stiles took a closer look at their pale flesh and wide, staring eyes. As the bus bounced along the street, the passengers wavered, but their bodies seemed locked into their seats.

The passengers were dead.

"Fuck," Stiles spat. He had to get off the bus.

He grabbed the metal rail behind him and kicked the bus driver directly in that frazzled, eggshell head. The driver lost control of the bus. The large transportation vehicle veered to the right and ran up the empty sidewalk, the tires squealing. Then, it caromed up the concrete embankment before finally flipping onto it left side. Stiles held on for his life as the world spun.

The passengers were laying every-which-way inside the bus, but Stiles didn't give a shit. His only thought was to get off the bus before it arrived at its final destination. Crawling to the center emergency window on the right side, he pulled up the red latch and pushed open the safety glass. He then squeezed through the opening and dropped down to the pavement. Moving around to the front of the bus, he caught the driver grinning at him through the window and flipped him off.

"No bus is taking me to hell!" his voice seemed to echo while he locked eyes with the maniacal bus driver.

What just happened? How drunk was he?

None of it mattered. In the morning, he would wake up in a pile of his own vomit, broke and helpless. He would have to win back his paycheck because the high cost of living couldn't wait on him.

The only thing that could correct the mistake was to scrape together some change and hit those machines again, and again. He was going to be a winner at some point. He couldn't possibly be *that* unlucky.

A bus full of dead people that was driving into hell? That was worth a laugh...

Stiles rushed across Tropicana Avenue, not bothering to look in either direction. A dull roar filled his head and he found it difficult to think. There didn't seem to be a soul on either side of the street. What was happening? He needed to lie down and sleep.

He never saw the Toyota that hit him, causing his body to fly through the air and to hit the asphalt twenty feet away with a cringing *thud*.

"Sir?" a voice insisted. "Sir?"

Stiles realized that he was aware, that he existed; he felt as if his head was submerged beneath water. He opened his eyes and stared up at the Blue Bayou security officer. He was inside the casino again.

"I'm afraid you can't sleep in the Race and Sports Book," the officer said. "Would you like me to send a cocktail waitress over to you with a cup of coffee?"

"No, that's okay," Stiles groaned and shielded his eyes from the glaring bright light.

The hellish carnival music produced by the multitude of slot machines suggested that he'd never left the place. It was nothing more than a bad dream. How could he have overpowered security officers in a moment of drunken bravado?

A bus to hell...?

"I need to be getting home," Stiles croaked.

"Yes, sir."

Stiles rose to his feet and took his wallet out from his back pocket and checked the inside. The money from his cashed paycheck was still there. He breathed a sigh of relief. He could still invest his money in the poker machines, but that would have to wait.

"Are you okay?" the officer asked.

"Just a bad dream," Stiles nodded, pleased with reality.

The officer walked away, leaving the gambler to rub sleep from his eyes.

Stiles walked through the casino and out the main door facing Tropicana. The sunlight was a little too much for him. He stood outside of the Bayou for a few moments to allow his eyes to adjust; everything seemed to be washed in white light.

The clouds above him seemed to race over the bright blue heaven above. The pedestrian traffic seemed to move languidly, with all eyes focused ahead.

Thankfully, he only lived about three blocks down from the casino. He cut through the front parking lot to the sidewalk and turned left. He decided to cross at the stoplight rather than jaywalk. After the eerie dream he'd had, he felt the need to play it safe and obey the law.

While Stiles waited for the red light to change at the intersection, he stood and watched a black bus approach, heading in an easterly direction toward the Strip.

He wanted to look away, but he felt like his feet were embedded into the concrete.

The bus driver glanced his way and offered him a huge smile. Stiles could see the black, oily stains on those large teeth as the bus began to slow. The driver's dreadful gaze remained on him; the heavy eyebrows sagged over gleeful eyes. Stiles recognized the face from his nightmare and felt goose bumps rise up on his arms.

"No!" he threw his head back and screamed.

The bright white clouds in the sky above seemed to darken and collide.

MR. DAMAGE

CHRISTOPHER NADEAU

When Mother keeled over and died in front of the window, Destiny wasn't surprised. Nor was she shaken up. She'd known the day was coming. Arsenic in apple pie will do that to a person, by and by.

She hadn't hated her mother. She couldn't remember a time when she'd wished for her death. The only thing that ever entered Destiny's mind was the image of her mother sitting in that silly chair, staring outside that silly window, until the dust and wind consumed them both.

Perhaps she'd felt sorry for the poor, aging thing who'd given up on life so long ago. The Catholic priest's words rang hollow in her mind now, anecdotal reminders of a hope that had died a harsh death. Mother never found the faith within herself to admit God's love back into her heart, and in so doing she'd killed it in her daughter's as well.

Destiny felt no animosity. So why did she do it?

Her mother named her Destiny when the world seemed to be on the brink of something truly special.

Then came the War to End All Wars, and everybody started wondering if progress came with too high a cost. Despite the lasting, traumatic effects the war seemed to have on everybody, good times arrived in a heedless rush of cash, drink, and music. Destiny came of age during this time and her optimism knew no limits.

Until Father, who'd served his country well in that nearly cataclysmic conflict, killed himself.

The doctors called it *shell-shock* and assured both Mother and Destiny he would get past it someday.

One day Father walked into the barn, they heard a popping noise, and he was dead.

Mother changed after that. She'd loved the Lord and was convinced He loved her as well until Father committed suicide.

How could a God she adored with all her heart allow the man she loved to return home from the war as a dim shadow of the man he used to be? No man of the cloth seemed able to offer a satisfactory answer, and before Destiny knew it, they'd stopped going to church.

Destiny didn't give up easily. She read the Bible nightly and talked to as many holy people as she could, lay followers and ministers alike. She even sneaked off and talked to a *Catholic priest.* She wouldn't have dared share this fact with Mother, remembering well her comments about those *deceived papists*, but Destiny figured maybe a man of the cloth from the oldest Christian church might have some answers.

Mother deteriorated as the years wore on. There were days she'd just sit before the window and stare out it, as if expecting Father to come wandering up the long driveway. Once, she let out a gasp so loud it caused Destiny to trip over the kitchen table and land hard on her left knee. That knee would never heal right and she'd walk with a limp for the rest of her life.

"What is it, Mother?" she said.

"I saw..." her mother began and then stopped as if thinking better of it. "Never mind what I saw."

Destiny might have questioned her if not for the excruciating pain in her knee. This was in the days before readily available ice; she used cold compresses on it. The next morning, Doc Lewis came over to help alleviate the swelling.

As the months wore on, Mother would throw fits, sometimes tossing objects around the house, until Destiny left her alone to sit in front of that damned window.

She'd long given up any hope of knowing why Mother stared through the window the day she finally told Destiny the reason. Mother had requested Destiny's apple pie, a recipe whose secret was closely guarded and jealously sought after by the ladies in town. Destiny happily indulged her. Anything that made Mother smile, even momentarily, was worth a few hours' work.

The pie was cooling on the opposite windowsill from where Mother always sat.

"It should be ready to eat in a few minutes, Mother."

"Wonderful, child. Your apple pie is always worth the wait."

Destiny felt tears in her eyes, forced a trembling smile, and walked over to stand beside her Mother.

"Do you still want to know what I see out there?" Mother said.

For a moment, Destiny thought she'd imagined what she heard.

Mother had a distant look in her eyes. "I see the King of the World looking back at me with a look that says he knows the answer."

Destiny leaned down and followed her mother's gaze out the window, seeing only an empty field. "The answer to what, Mother?"

"Why we suffer, honey." She stood up from her chair and stepped around Destiny. "Now, let's go have some of that lovely apple pie before the folks in town catch a whiff and come a'runnin'."

The Great Depression hit the small towns even harder than the big cities. If you didn't have a farm or a business that could survive on trade, you were most likely wandering the Earth in search of work. Destiny was fortunate in the beginning because of the crops she was able to grow, but when the Dust Bowl made it to her home, the top soil left with the wind and her dreams.

Mother still stared through her window, but the dust and the wind concealed the scoured land, leaving scant inches of bare field. In spite of that, she never gave up on seeing whatever she thought was out there.

Destiny tried her best to live some sort of a life. She wasn't the prettiest woman in town but she had suitors. Sadly, none of them ever seemed to want to deal with Mother once they saw what she was like. Soon, they stopped coming altogether.

Destiny gave up hope of ever leaving her home, with its horrible memories and maddening repetitiveness. Her name became the very thing she wished she could change.

The remaining townsfolk arrived at Mother's funeral as if it were the social event of the season. Miserable, hungry, restless individuals came and paid their respects as if they'd been waiting for something to remind them that their lives weren't all that bad after all.

Destiny received them with grace and decorum, traits instilled in her as a child by the woman whose dead body rested below ground. People assured her they would be checking in on her from time to time. Imagine, they said, that poor girl living alone with no man to take care of her.

Their good intentions lasted about six weeks before they slowly trickled away to occasional stop-ins by the ladies of the church social groups. It was nice to finally be alone.

Sometimes she would awake to the sound of Mother's voice, perhaps only a clearing of the throat or a tiny cough. She'd walk into Mother's room and remind herself Mother was dead. She told herself she would get rid of Mother's bed, possibly even burn it.

Other times, while she was sewing or reading one of the dime novels she purchased at an estate sale, she swore she heard Mother's chair creaking as if someone sat in it. One night, she decided to sit there and look out the window and see what was so all-fired fascinating.

Sitting in Mother's chair, staring out at nothing lost its appeal rather quickly.

By now even the church ladies had ceased to come. There was no greater sin in a small town than refusal to step foot inside a house of worship, for it was well known that those who refused to do so had turned their backs on the Lord.

Destiny held no hatred for God, but she saw no point in following Him, either. Never once did it occur to her to think God might not exist.

Destiny never questioned the existence or nature of God, until the stranger arrived.

At first she thought the dust storm must surely have created an illusion. She gasped and shot to her feet, running to grab Father's shotgun from the pantry. Although it hadn't been used in years, Destiny had kept it nice and oiled the way she'd been taught.

By the time she'd loaded and cocked it, there was a knock at the door. It was a weak knock, the kind one heard from ailing elderly folks or timid children. Certainly not what she'd expect from a healthy young man.

"Who's there?" she called.

"'Evening, ma'am," came the muted reply. "I was wondering if you had a room for rentin'."

Destiny frowned. The answer was no, but perhaps it wasn't such a bad idea. She needed to know if this man was a derelict or not.

"Perhaps," she said. "How much are you looking to spend?"

"Ma'am, for a soft bed and some running water, I'd spend five dollars a night!"

Destiny licked her chapped lips. That was good money, assuming he had it. "I've got a gun," she said.

The man chuckled. "Okay, how about six dollars then?"

In spite of herself, Destiny chuckled as well. The sound was foreign to her. Against her better judgment, she walked over and opened the door, stepping back enough to keep the shotgun leveled at the stranger. His appearance shocked her.

If he was a young man, his impairments made it impossible to judge his true age. His face was gaunt, his eyes sunken, his flesh gray and covered with blemishes. He had a full head of hair that seemed to sprout from the center and lay on top like a poorly-designed hat. As her gaze tracked downward, she noticed how incredibly thin he was. His clothing was baggy and looked as if it hadn't been cleaned in ages, while his shoes were mere coverings over his feet, worn and ready to burst open at any moment. She took a step back as he raised what remained of his right arm; only half of it was left.

The worst thing she could imagine him doing to her was dying on her front porch.

When he smiled, he revealed a row of crooked, yellowing teeth that looked like they were ready to tumble out of his mouth like jagged pieces of rice.

"Do we have a deal?" he asked.

Destiny nodded slowly and lowered the shotgun.

Why did she feel as if she'd just given up a part of herself she would never get back?

The man said he didn't remember his name, where he came from, or what he'd done before the Depression started.

"Truth to tell, ma'am, I don't have much memory of the days before it, either," he said.

He spoke of time crunching together, becoming a mist that covered you but never showed you the way forward or back. Something about that description spoke to her.

"Well, I just have to call you something," she said, not unkindly.

The man stopped setting the table for dinner and glanced up, his gaze far away and filled with regret, sadness, or perhaps a mixture of the two.

"The fellas on the train used to call me *Mr. Damage*, on account of my condition."

Destiny's hand went to her mouth. "My goodness, what a simply dreadful thing to call someone."

The man shrugged. "Different breed of folks, ma'am."

"I am not going to call you by that awful nickname."

"Oh, I don't mind it none. Gives me character and such." He sat down for a moment and rubbed his severed arm. "A man needs character in these troubled times."

Destiny smiled. "As does a woman. I'll call you Mr. D and nothing more."

Mr. D looked up and smiled his toothy, rotted gum smile. "Suits me just fine, Miss Destiny."

It didn't take long for the man the 'fellas' on the train called Mr. Damage to become part of Destiny's life. Not only did he pay his room and board faithfully every Friday by noon, he also helped out around the place and made whatever repairs a one-armed man could manage. She couldn't have asked for a more respectful roomer, but no amount of respectability could ever convince the nosey biddies from her church there wasn't serious hanky-panky afoot.

They made regular Saturday visits, arms filled with baskets of food, eyes filled with merciless judgment. She always received them with friendly greetings and sent them away without a single new piece of information to share with the other vultures.

She supposed it was inevitable one of them would run into Mr. D. All it took was a change in their routine, and they discovered the man himself outside painting the long, white picket fence that ran the length of the driveway.

The church ladies were thrilled. Contrary to what Destiny expected, they seemed to find him delightful. She supposed he was a charmer, and frankly, she was a tad jealous.

"Dear, you simply *must* bring your roomer to church this Sunday," Velma Kincaid said.

"I'm not sure Mr. D is much for church, Velma." Destiny heard the lack of conviction in her voice and hated the sound of it.

"Nonsense, dear!" Velma placed her hands on her ample hips. "Why, he just finished telling us about his baptism. He even quoted a few lines of scripture."

Destiny frowned; Mr. D had never mentioned God, Jesus, or the Bible in the months he'd been rooming with her. She'd assumed he was one of those atheists. She told Velma she would ask him later when he was finished with the fence.

"Why not ask him now?" Before Destiny could protest, Velma turned her ample frame away from her and yelled for Mr. D.

"Ma'am?" he yelled back.

"We would be thrilled to have you in church with us this coming Sunday."

A look crossed his face for the briefest of moments, almost like a shadow of indecision and fear. It vanished so quickly, Destiny told herself it was the midday sun, but doubts lingered.

"Yes, ma'am," he said. "We'll be there."

Velma turned back around and smiled triumphantly at Destiny. "See you Sunday, dear."

Destiny stared at the back of Velma's head as she commanded her chubby followers to bid Mr. D a fond farewell. As they drove off, she thought, *You deserve whatever you get.*

She had no idea where that thought came from.

That Sunday started innocently enough, with Mr. D fussing over the suit he'd bought in town, complaining that it was both too tight and too loose. She found herself enjoying this most human moment with a man and talked him through it as best she could. She, on the other hand, wore the clothes she always wore to church: a simple print dress that came to the ankle. She had no intention of putting on airs.

During the drive to church, she couldn't help noticing Mr. D's nervousness. He fidgeted in his seat and kept glancing through the window as if expecting something to grab him at any moment. She considered asking what was wrong and thought better of it. Men like Mr. D had demons in their past. Lord only knew what going to church reminded the poor man of.

She remained silent.

Their arrival at church was eagerly anticipated. Destiny waited patiently for Mr. D to get out of the Studebaker and walk around to her side and open the door. He seemed to take forever while she sat there, trying not to stare back at the assembled churchgoers currently aligning the narrow walkway leading inside

"Thank you," she said just loud enough to be overheard by those closest to them.

The first group they encountered included Stanley Jamison and his children (Mrs. Jamison had died the previous summer) and Mrs. Wilkes, the widow who owned the largest farm in town. Although they were two very different people, they both reacted to the arrival of Mr. D, with a strange mixture of hesitancy and revulsion. They were both excellent at concealing their reactions, as most small-town folks are, but Destiny could see it in their eyes.

Following awkward introductions and pleasantries, she and Mr. D moved deeper into the crowd until they encountered the chubby church ladies. Velma Kincaid greeted them with a maddeningly wide smile, her fat arms widened as well as if she were going to run across an empty field and scoop up her lover. Destiny glanced at Mr. D, whose blank expression gave away nothing of what he was feeling inside. She felt sorry for this poor man, a disfigured angel trying to get along in a world that continually looked for reasons to point and stare at him.

Well, he had a friend now.

"You came!" Velma said. "I was *hoping* you would!"

"We said we would, ma'am," he said with the slightest hint of irritation.

Velma froze, looking very much like an overweight crucifix with her arms still held out. The moment passed almost as quickly as it began, however, and she returned to her previous bluster.

Destiny waited with false patience for Velma to return with her roomer.

"Here we are, dear," Velma said. "Hope I didn't keep you two apart too long?"

Destiny smiled. "We're rarely together, I'm afraid. Mr. D has his chores and I have mine."

"Goodness, such a shame." Velma shook her head. "Perhaps you two will get better reacquainted during Reverend Felcher's sermon."

Velma spun on her heels and walked inside, the other church ladies in quick lockstep behind her. Destiny apologized to Mr. D, who assured her there was no reason to do. They started towards the entrance when Destiny remembered that her purse was still in the car.

"I'd simply leave it but I won't be able to leave anything in the collection plate if I don't have..."

"I'll get it for you, ma'am."

She watched Mr. D trot away to the car, his limp seeming off somehow. What was different about it? Didn't he normally limp on his right foot?

"Somethin' off about that one."

Destiny turned in time to see Jesse Barker standing next to her. He looked worse since the days they'd courted; he was somehow diminished.

"I beg your pardon?" she said.

Jesse shrugged. "None of my business, of course. Just passin' the time."

Destiny glanced over to see Mr. D bent inside the car.

"You just keep a real close eye on him in church," Jesse said. He walked away before she could question him.

Mr. D reappeared a moment later with her purse, a quizzical expression on his face.

"Shall we?" Destiny offered him her arm.

Together, they entered the church.

Jesse Barker was known for having a talent. He wasn't particularly bright but sometimes he just...knew things.

That was what caused Destiny to put a halt to their courtship so early on. That and his horrible breath.

Folks around town said Jesse Barker had the sight, meaning he was touched with special powers. Others considered such talk to be devilment and would have none of it in their presence.

The first time he'd come calling was shortly after her mother's death.

"You shouldn't feel too bad about what you done," he said one night.

They'd been sitting in her parlor, sipping ice tea and looking up at the stars, wondering if they shone on happier places. She looked up from her glass into Jesse's simple eyes and frowned.

"She was ready to go," he said.

Destiny said nothing. She merely stared at him until he looked away and then got to her feet. With a brief, "Good night," she ushered him to the door and went to bed, where she didn't sleep a wink.

That was the last time she saw him...until today.

As she and Mr. D sat in the middle row, Jesse's words from both that night and a few moments before echoed in her head. Why did she need to keep an eye on Mr. D? She glanced at her roomer and noted the beads of sweat on his forehead and the way his mouth seemed to twitch involuntarily. His stump moved up and down as if an invisible hand sat at the end, clenching over and over. Destiny leaned over and asked him if he was all right.

"Truth to tell, ma'am, I am feeling a bit poorly," he said.

"Should we leave?" She asked in a way that only the simplest person wouldn't have heard the implied reluctance in her tone.

Mr. D smiled wanly. "No, ma'am This here's important."

Destiny gave an uncertain nod and sat back with a light sigh. She could feel everyone's eyes on her, coming from all directions at once. She ignored the hot feeling at the back of her head and chose to focus on the arrival of Reverend Felcher, whose scowling face brought back all sorts of unpleasant memories of the past. Until he showed up, she'd almost forgotten why she didn't come here anymore.

"Good morning, my brothers and sisters," he said in his deep, affected intonation.

Mr. D rubbed his palm on his leg over and over.

"I stand before you today a renewed man," Reverend Felcher said, "for I was given a vision this past week that cleared up many of the doubts you, my congregation, have had of late."

Mr. D stopped rubbing his palm and looked up at the Reverend with full attention and focus. Destiny glanced about the room at the doe-eyed townsfolk sitting around them. They hung on the reverend's every word, as if missing something would damn them to eternal fire and torment. How she despised them in that instant, with their simplistic, provincial approach to the Divine. How she wanted to get up and spin on her heels and stomp out of there with or without Mr. Damage.

But a lifetime of conditioning froze her to the spot.

"I was working on my new deck when it happened, brothers and sisters."

Mr. D snorted. Destiny shook her head; what poor taste to mention his fancy new home in the midst of all this suffering. Even worse was the fact that church donations had funded his beloved deck.

"Mrs. Felcher was in the kitchen making her sinfully delicious lemonade at the time." This comment drew the chuckles it was designed to win. "And there I was, securing a wood beam, when a sharp pain entered my head, like a headache that came from *outside* of me!"

Mr. D smirked as much of the congregation emitted a simultaneous gasp.

Reverend Felcher went on to describe his experience as a blinding flash of light behind his eyes. He fell to his knees, dropped his hammer, and tried to call out for his wife. He said he felt that he was yelling her name over and over, but Mrs. Felcher heard nothing.

Then a voice spoke to him, at once soothing and commanding.

"And I knew it was a voice from Heaven." Felcher paused, his hands held out and up in supplication of God's mercy. "Perhaps not the Almighty, but certainly one of His emissaries."

Mr. D lowered his head and leaned forward as if to say, "Go on. What next?"

"And the voice spoke unto me, brothers and sisters. It told me not to worry, that these troubled times were a test not of us, but of the Devil himself!"

A hush fell over the congregation. Destiny heard a few whispered comments, but they were too low for her to make out specifically what was said. This new wrinkle in the search for why we suffer gripped everyone, including her.

"That's right." Felcher banged his fist on the podium. "The Lord's messenger told me that we stand at the precipice of a choice. The Devil still hath dominion over this world and he demands his due!"

No one in the congregation moved a muscle. They were all statues for Christ, awaiting the order to react to divine revelation.

"We are in the middle and we must make our choice," Felcher said, his voice growing with each word. "Our destiny is at hand, brothers and sisters! Are we going to let the Devil defeat us?"

No! they all cried.

"Are we going to choose the Lord?"

Yes!

Felcher smiled. "We suffer because Satan suffers. The Son of God changed the rules and now he resents being so diminished. I say...We diminish him until he is powerless! Praise the Lord! Amen!"

Amen! Amen!

Destiny felt removed from the moment, separate from the mass of exhorting church-goers. She looked over at Mr. D and noticed him coughing into his hand. Or was he *laughing*? She didn't experience the hope that encircled the room. She still wanted to leave, perhaps now more than ever.

Right on cue, the collection plate started making its round, two ushers standing at the ends of each aisle as members dropped coins, dollars, and promissory notes into the baskets to the accompaniment of some standard gospel tune being sung with utter sincerity by the choir. Mr. D leaned over and whispered into Destiny's ear, "You don't have to if you don't want, ma'am."

She looked at him as if he'd lost his mind. To attend a church service and not donate...well, it was unthinkable.

Destiny watched the plate move quickly along the people in the row in front of theirs and sighed. She opened her purse and rummaged around inside for whatever coins she could find. The plate came to her and she dropped all of them in, passing it to her right. Mr. D took the plate and held it for a few seconds, staring down into it as if seeing something only he could understand. Someone tapped on Destiny's shoulder, causing her to turn her head. Oddly, no one reacted when she turned around. She turned back to face her roomer, who had by now passed the plate to the row behind them.

It took a few more minutes before both plates were handed back to the ushers and taken back to the front of the church. The choir continued a bit longer, Mrs. Madison belting about the words, "Praise the Lord," while Mrs. Jenkins tortured the poor church organ with her usual carelessness. Destiny flinched as the two women arrived at the final note of the song with a combination of whininess and atonal assault on the senses.

"As always, those ladies remind us of the reason we congregate to worship the Lord," Reverend Felcher said. "Such beautiful sounds were designed to glorify God."

Mr. D snorted and started coughing, causing Destiny to cover her mouth and stare at the back of the bench in front of her. How inappropriate, she thought, to laugh in church when no one else was. This thought served to make refraining from laughter even more difficult.

"Thank you so much to all who gave an offering today," the reverend continued. "It's greatly appreciated in these hard times, brothers and sisters." He bent down to pick up one of the baskets. "Here is Christian charity at its finest! Even those who have nothing have vowed to give when they can." He wiped his dry eyes as if a tear fell from them and opened a few of the notes. "Such wonderful, loving, giving...*who the hell wrote this*?"

A collective gasp went up from the congregation as Felcher stepped from around his podium and shook the offending note. "Who found this funny? Who think it's funny to make such blasphemous and filthy accusations of a man of God?"

Everyone looked around, as if in so doing they would discover the perpetrator of whatever outrage had caused their spiritual father to curse in the middle of his sermon.

"How dare someone make such a claim!"

Velma Kincaid jumped up from her spot near the front and ran up to the Reverend before he could react. "What does the note say, Reverend?"

Felcher, for the first time realizing what he was doing, cleared his throat and said, "Well, now sister Velma, I suppose I shouldn't have allowed my anger to..."

"Nonsense, Reverend!" She grabbed the paper from him and read it, emitting a gasp that echoed throughout the church. "Goodness me!"

Felcher forced a smile. "It's obviously a childish prank."

"What does it say?" someone demanded.

Destiny glanced over and realized it was Mr. D.

Velma made a sound of utter horror and revulsion that was contradicted by the ever-widening smile on her face. "Some prankster wrote, 'Why didn't you tell the congregation that you weren't working on your deck? You were...*pleasuring yourself!*"

A cacophony of shocked gasps, derisive laughter, reluctant amusement, and God knew what else filled the room, rising and falling in crescendo. Reverend Felcher seemed to shrink before Destiny's eyes until his formerly stern persona became that of a frightened child desperate to avoid its punishment. Velma, ever the actress, pretended to faint at Felcher's feet, the note still miraculously held aloft for the next person to grab it.

"That's what it says, all right," said the man who held it next.

The note made its way through the now standing congregation like some mockery of a collection plate, each member glancing at it, verbalizing their disgust and moving it down the line. Children were rushed out of the building, their parents yelling at them to stop asking what "pleasuring yourself" meant. The identity of the note's author became a moot point as everyone focused on the terrible sin of Reverend Felcher, the hypocrite and degenerate.

"Reverend Felcher, how could you?" a woman shrieked from the back of the church.

"We'd better leave, ma'am," Mr. D said.

Destiny turned on him sharply, ready to demand some answers, but one look at his stooped posture and stump caused her to immediately lose the urge. Without a word, she rose and followed him as he weaved through the crowded church, expertly avoiding touching anyone as he went. To her surprise, they saw Reverend Felcher standing before the entrance, his arms held outward as if ready to be nailed to a cross.

"Please do not believe these base accusations, brothers and sisters!" he yelled. "Satan is alive and well in the hearts of the awful prankster who..."

Mr. D leaned forward and whispered something in the reverend's ear that caused him to stop emoting and freeze in place, his eyes bugging out while his jaw slackened. When he did finally speak, it was at such a low register that Destiny couldn't make it out. She tried reading his lips instead, frowning at him as she attempted to comprehend what he was mouthing. Mr. D motioned for her to follow him out the doors.

On their way to the car, she demanded to know what he had said to the reverend that caused him such distress.

Mr. D shrugged in his self-conscious way. "Nothin' that should have upset him too terrible, ma'am. Just told him I was with him."

Mr. D walked around the Studebaker and got in on the passenger side without another word, while Destiny stared after him. What did that mean? And what did it have to do with what Reverend Felcher was saying?

She was pretty sure she'd heard the spellbound minister mumble, "The voice, the voice."

Weeks passed uneventfully on Destiny's farm. Crops died while some were saved. The house was fully repaired, thanks to her roomer. A few men came by looking for room and board but seemed to lose interest when they met Mr. D. She chalked this up to their own prejudices towards the disfigured, but sometimes she was unable to fully convince herself of this. Soon, no one came to visit anymore.

The news she gathered from town wasn't good for Reverend Felcher or anybody else. The righteous reverend, unable to prove the allegations of his self-pleasuring, had packed up and left town. A rotating roster of visiting men of the cloth ran services there. Without the steadying influence of Felcher, attendance was down. Besides, things were getting worse anyway. More and more people were coming down with illnesses or leaving town in search of whatever work they could find.

Destiny didn't really care. Her life was over long ago, and now the only thing keeping her going was curiosity. She spent every day following the incident at church, trying to figure out a way to broach the subject of what really happened.

As it turned out, Mr. D brought it up one night while they were sitting in the living room, having tea.

"What'd you think of the reverend's sermon, ma'am?" he asked.

This was the first time she could remember him ever asking her a question of any relevance, and it took a moment for her to process this.

Mr. D nodded absently.

"I'd certainly never heard that concept of the Devil before, had you?"

Mr. D smiled. "Yes, ma'am."

Destiny's eyebrow rose into a V. "You've heard the *Devil* is being tested instead of Man?"

"Ain't quite that simple." He drained his tea and leaned forward to pour more into his cup when Destiny intercepted and filled it for him. "People are being tested as well, but the real test don't start unless the Devil fails."

Destiny's hand shook as she tried to pick up her tea cup and placed it gently back on the saucer. "I don't remember reading anything in the Bible about that."

Mr. D shook his head. "No, ma'am, and you ain't never gonna. That ain't a story for the everyday folks."

Destiny forced a chuckle. "Why, Mr. D, I swear you sound like you know of these things firsthand."

A shadow seemed to cross his face then, a darkness that changed his features until he no longer appeared as the helpless, disfigured soul she'd pitied so. "Mayhap I do." He drank from his coffee cup and let out a long sigh. "Mayhap I do."

Destiny placed her tea cup and saucer on the table with an audible clank. "I have no interest in this sort of talk! I would prefer that we discuss something else or bid each other a good night!"

Mr. D set his cup down on the table and glanced to his left. "You keep your mama's chair sittin' there like when I first come here."

Momentarily taken aback, Destiny found herself responding before she could tell herself to remain silent. "I like to keep a memory of my mother."

Mr. D smirked. "A chair for mama and a shotgun for daddy, eh?"

Before she could say anything, he had already gotten to his feet and walked over to her mother's chair. "You keep this here because you think one day you'll sit in it and see what she saw."

Destiny allowed her arms to go slack at her sides as she followed his sudden pacing.

Mr. D no longer seemed to be speaking with the Deep South accent he'd exhibited all these months.

He smiled. "I'm what she saw."

She remembered Mother saying: "*I see the King of the World looking back at me with a look that says he knows the answer.*"

Destiny stared down at the floor, unwilling or perhaps even unable to look into the eyes of the man standing before her. What would she see if she looked up? What would change?

"Don't you want to know why we suffer?" he asked.

Her voice shaky, Destiny informed him she wasn't interested in anything he had to say. Whatever silly tricks he was pulling, whatever those fat idiot women at church had put him up to, it was over now.

He sighed and sat back down. "We suffer because God is insane."

Destiny grabbed her tea cup and saucer and hurled it across the room, smashing it into pieces against the front door. "That is *enough*! Get out!"

Mr. D continued as if she hadn't spoken. "I first reached that conclusion a long, long time ago, ma'am. Doing so sealed my fate forever."

This time Destiny did look up, her expression filled with fury as her nostrils flared. "That's blasphemy, and I will ask you one more time to get..."

"God punishes them that question His will." He held up his missing arm and smirked.

Destiny's anger slipped away then, replaced by a hysterical amusement. "Oh, you poor man. You're blaming God for your unfortunate condition."

Mr. D sat back and stared off into space. "He ripped it right off."

Something about his tone forced her into an uneasy silence. Despite her reluctance, a strong part of her wanted to hear what he had to say.

"Can you think of anything worse than being separated from your purpose?" he said, staring at his stump. "Mayhap not being able to die. Mayhap that's worse. Put the two together and pretty soon hate becomes your only companion. Then you don't know if you're filled with it or if it's just what you are."

"A...are you filled with hate?" she stammered.

Smiling wide, he said, "Yes, ma'am! Hate for this wicked old world and the hypocrites that infest it like cockroaches on a piece of rancid meat. Hate for the people that read an edited Bible and think it ultimate truth. Hate for this twisted form I wear as I walk the Earth, empty and hollowed out." He poured himself another cup of tea and took a sip. "But sometimes love can still take place." He looked at her and winked.

Destiny shot to her feet, instinctively heading for Mother's chair at the window. Her breaths coming in short, quick inhalations and exhalations, she shook her head over and over. "Mr. D, I don't know what you expect from me, but I'm not..."

"Relax, ma'am." He got to his feet and faced her. "What I love is the choice you've been given."

Destiny forced a smile. "I have no idea what you're talking about."

"No, ma'am. Of course not." He took a few steps towards her. "How could you?"

She felt as if this thing, whatever it was, was a secret she already knew and had simply forgotten. It nagged at her, *gnawed* at her, like something concealed for far too long suddenly demanding its moment out in the open.

Mr. D asked her to retake her seat and waited while she did so. Draining his tea cup, he sat down and once again faced her, his expression grave. "Ma'am, I've been waiting for this moment for a long, long time."

She noticed his previous speech pattern had returned. Destiny motioned for him to continue.

"Have you ever heard of a plea bargain?"

She nodded. "I listen to the suspense shows on the radio."

His smile was disturbingly affectionate. "'Course you do." He told her that plea bargain was as close a concept as he could get to what had occurred so long ago between him and the Lord. God, furious over his daring to question His will, had banished him from the heavenly realms and threatened to toss him into what Mr. D referred to as the "Great Emptiness."

"That ain't a place you wanna wind up," he said. "Worse than any Hell men can imagine."

Mr. D said God agreed to spare him that fate, but decreed that he would be sentenced to wander the Earth forever until the End

Times. Things changed with the so-called "Age of Grace," during which Man was given a second chance.

"My world was taken from me," Mr. D said matter-of-factly. "It occurred to me that this had been God's plan all along."

"When the Son was born, I had no choice but to seek him out."

In his version, Mr. D had approached the Son not to corrupt him but to enlist his aid. The Son would not hear of it. Mr. D's dominion was reduced and he was given a new edict to follow.

"I was told that one day a human would come and that human would be given a choice."

Destiny forced herself to blink. "What choice?"

Mr. D smiled. "Interesting that you didn't ask me which human." He poured himself another cup of tea and sat back. "I've been so busy trying to show the people that God doesn't care about them but nothing I do seems to affect fanatics like Reverend Felcher one little old bit."

The voice, Destiny thought. Reverend Felcher was talking about the voice of Heaven he claimed told him about the Devil.

"People need miracles, Destiny," he said. "I gave them one."

"Good Lord Almighty," she whispered into her hand.

"You have no idea how hard it was sitting in that wretched shithole, excuse my French. He hasn't made it easy for me to enter His little homes away from home. But I persevere because Mankind must know the truth. Even if we lose, at least we can..." He paused and drank some tea. "I lost my arm when he cast me out. I was reaching back, begging Him to forgive me, when the gates closed on my arm." He chuckled bitterly.

"You're insane," Destiny said.

"Probably." He glanced over at the chair and grinned. "I whispered in your mother's ear the reason for all suffering, and she still wanted to know more. But it wasn't for her to know. Your name is no accident, sweet Destiny."

"Insane," Destiny said with awe in her voice.

"Jesse was right. She was ready to go."

Destiny leapt from the couch and slapped him hard enough to draw blood. Mr. D wiped his finger along the cut in his thin lip and held it up for her to see. "Hate travels in the blood."

"GET OUT! GET OUT OF MY HOUSE!"

Mr. D reached out with a quickness he'd never before displayed and grabbed hold of Destiny's wrist so tightly she felt the blood draining from it.

"Sit down and hear the rest," he said in an eerily calm tone.

She didn't notice herself sitting until she looked up and saw him looming over her.

"Do you know why you poisoned her, Destiny?"

"She was already dead." she said coldly.

"You did it because you thought you could change your fate. Just like me, you thought you could challenge the way things were and break away from it."

She saw the truth in his words and held back. She hated him for knowing this about her.

"It isn't a sin when everything has already been set up for a specific outcome," he said.

"What do you want from me?" she asked.

"Faith."

She looked away. "If you know what I did, then you know God isn't..."

"Not in God! In *me*. I need you to believe my story. Can you do that?"

Destiny bit her bottom lip and sighed. "What will happen if I don't?"

Mr. D hung his head. "The world will get worse. Darkness will fall over all lands. Wars the likes of which you've never seen, incurable diseases, children murdering their parents and each other. Corruption. Death by the millions. Everything will unravel."

"You're telling me it will all be my fault?"

Mr. D shrugged. "That depends on your point of view, I suppose."

Destiny looked at this misshapen man, this lost soul, and did indeed feel pity for a sad little man desperate to matter in a world that didn't care about him.

"I don't believe you," she said.

The look on his face was a heartbreaking combination of shock and dismay. He stumbled backwards a bit, nearly falling over her coffee table until he righted himself. His face contorted and twitched as if many voices dueled for dominance within him.

"Your name should have been Pandora," he said, "considering what you've unleashed."

"I'm sorry," she said. "I know you believe it, but I think you're a very sick man."

He walked toward the door and paused with his hand on the knob.

The years passed slowly as the Great Depression became worse. Before she knew it, the country had been attacked and was in the midst of a conflict unlike any in history, a real World War. The death and devastation seemed unreal and still she told herself it was all coincidence.

Then the U.S. dropped two atomic bombs on Japan and she started losing sleep. More wars, more deaths.

She closed all her doors and windows and drew the blinds.

Some distant part of her said that Mr. D's so-called 'choice' had been the ranting of a crazy man, but she didn't care anymore.

Soon she would be gone, just like Mother.

Arsenic in apple pie will do that to a person, by and by.

BE MINE FOREVER

M. L. TRAXLER

John went straight home after work as usual and flopped down on the soiled, torn recliner which had been left outside on trash day by a neighbor but was now inside his home. The only other pieces of furniture in the room was a leather couch that was so worn it had bald spots and duct tape where John had covered a few ripped areas, plus a small TV stand holding an old television he'd owned since he was a kid. Completing the living room furnishings was a sturdy, scuffed coffee table that was shoved up below the window, a goldfish bowl on top of it.

He sat unmoving, like a spindly pine that had taken root in the dilapidated recliner. John stared blankly for hours at the TV. Occasionally he would get up and fiddle with the loosely-fitting knob, changing channels to something that held his interest. The remote had stopped working last year, and he hadn't bothered getting another one. He should have bought a new TV, which he could afford because he'd been squirreling away money in a coffee can. Maybe he'd take a nice vacation with that money, perhaps a cruise. Besides, the television had been a gift from his aunt and he didn't want to lose anything that reminded him of his beloved Aunt Ruby.

When the window darkened with the day's departure, John pushed himself up wearily, then crossed the small, dingy apartment to the table below the dirty window. He looked down at the large goldfish bowl. It wasn't a *real* goldfish bowl, not really. He hadn't bought it, but instead had created it.

John had found a large jar at a flea market that had once held pickles or something similar in days gone by. The mouth was big enough that he could have stuck his head inside it, and the wide opening had given him plenty of room to work on setting up the 'bowl' like he'd wanted. John had decorated it with the requisite plastic seaweed, pirate's chest and a faux cave where the fish could hide. The rocks on the bottom were blue; he was pleased with the goldfish jar.

He'd purchased several small comets and a large one, and then on a whim a bloated fancy goldfish with draping fins. First one, then the other smaller fish had disappeared within a few days. John wasn't sure which big fish was responsible until he noticed that the fancy one looked fatter than ever. He was tempted to catch it and flush it down the toilet, but one thing stayed his hand.

He'd been trying to train the fish from the first night to come for food when he tapped the side of the glass. Only the fancy one had responded, opening its mouth eagerly as John dropped flakes into the water. So, when the large comet's tail began to look ragged, he simply moved it to a bowl by itself. The poor thing died a few days later, but the fancy goldfish swam on as if nothing had happened to interrupt its days.

John sprinkled food onto the water and smiled wryly down at his goldfish Charlie. The goldfish was a cannibal all right, but was still a cool pet. The fish seemed to eye John happily as he fed. The food was a necessity for Charlie's existence, just as the goldfish was a necessary solace for John's isolation. Of course, Charlie didn't give him the friendship of a human, but it was companion-ship nonetheless.

John spoke quietly to his roommate, telling Charlie about his day as a cashier at the local grocery store. These moments with his pet were the brightest parts of John's day. Sure, people said hello to John at work and knew his name, but he couldn't talk to them. Not in a conversational way at least. He knew they thought he was that *odd, quiet man.* John always had trouble talking to people, whether it was men or women.

Being raised by an elderly aunt had left its mark on him. But he loved Aunt Ruby with a fierce loyalty, even though neighbors made remarks about her never having anyone over, or her strange way of talking to herself. Her death some years ago had created a dark void in his life, causing a deeper withdrawal into solitude.

Besides, how could he ever hope to connect with women? His tall, boney body, protruding eyes, and thick bush of hair that refused to lie down, no matter how much he combed it, made him unattractive to the fairer sex.

What would I say to women anyway? Nothing witty or profound. And it seemed too much trouble to try and fit in with the men at work. John's cloistered life had excluded sports and other manly pursuits, so he often felt like an alien from another planet when he heard men speaking about topics he didn't comprehend.

Sometimes, as he stared out at the nightlife through his grimy window, he felt as confined as his goldfish. *Charlie never changes,* he thought. *Just like me. Day after day he swims in his solitary prison— breathing in oxygen, defecating, and eating—so he can refuel and dirty the water again.*

When Charlie swam round and round the circumference of his world, John saw his life going on in a relentless circle of sameness.

The goldfish was graceful, beautiful, and he had John to care for him. That's where the similarities ended. At times John sensed his entire life was on pause, waiting for something to happen.

The next day, after work, John ambled into the neighborhood bar for a cold beer. He couldn't face his empty apartment just yet. It was a humid day, the kind that made his hair stand up in even more crazy patches.

John sipped the frothy beer and carried on a mundane conversation with the bartender, mostly responding to the man's statements. A woman entered the bar, swishing past him and taking the stool two down from him. Her perfume invaded his senses even after she'd passed him, drifting along behind her like a strong wind pulls leaves along in its wake. John and practically every male in the place eyed her speculatively. She wasn't a young woman, but still attractive in an overblown fashion.

Her lipstick was a bright pink shade, lighting up her lower face. Her skirt was tight and short, showing off a pair of meaty, but still shapely legs. Her breasts were large, the kind that drew men's eyes involuntarily. John didn't mind the slight bulge of flesh that pushed against her form-fitting sweater above the waistband.

She laughed gaily at a flirtatious remark made by the bartender, riveting the eyes and ears of every man. She drew them in with the lively sound of her banter and throaty laugh. Cocking her head slightly, she suddenly stared boldly at John, seeming to assess him from head to toe. With the grace of a jungle cat, sleek and confident, she stood up and slid onto the stool next to him.

"Hi. My name's Miranda." She stuck out a hand formally, but the breathy way she spoke belied the coolness of her introduction.

"John," he stuttered, blushing to the roots of his wildly disordered hair. He couldn't help but notice that not a strand was out of place in her carefully coiffed hair. He never understood how it happened, but not long after their introduction, he and Miranda were ensconced in his apartment. She sat gracefully in his recliner, draping her legs over one arm of the chair, then asked for a drink.

John hurriedly grabbed two nice glasses from the cabinet; wine goblets he'd bought on a whim at a garage sale while dreaming of a moment such as this. He ran them under the faucet, wiping them clean of the clinging dust that had collected in their three years on the shelf.

As he nervously splashed beer into both, he wondered if Miranda was the magic that would change his life. The several dates he'd had with a co-worker who was as shy as he suddenly seemed meaningless. He and Miranda had really connected in a way he couldn't fathom yet.

They talked for a while, about things he immediately forgot. His attention was captured by the wild beauty that exuded from her heavily-stacked body and hot eyes. She seemed to be searing a fiery path to his heart with those looks.

Abruptly, as if pulled by something outside himself, John was standing in front of the recliner, and then he was being wrapped in her strong arms. He groaned. The thrust of her bountiful breasts dug into his chest, making him hard in seconds.

She grabbed his head, pulling him forward, and then her tongue dove into his mouth. Miranda's tongue twined around his as tightly as her arms, and John moaned into her mouth, still in disbelief. She was in his apartment, in his arms. Even as her hands roamed over his back, setting up quivers of excitement, he clutched her to him in a desperate grip.

Like a parody of the x-rated movies he often watched alone, they began to frantically undress each other. John heard buttons pop off his shirt as she tugged at his clothes, but he didn't care.

Later, John lay contentedly beside his new love—his first lover. A fluttering feeling of pride flowed through him. Miranda had *screamed* in pleasure! He didn't know a lot about sex, not personally, but he'd always discounted the lunging, screaming women on porno films as Hollywood make-believe.

They'd had sex several times. He'd been hesitant at first, but Miranda was a patient lover, showing him how to do things correctly. Now, after their last session, Miranda lay quietly next to him. She had withdrawn a short space, but was still close enough that he could smell her perfume mixed with her own, womanly musky odor.

The bed creaked. He looked up in surprise as she stood up and walked nude towards the kitchen. "I'm going to get us a drink, you silly boy."

An embarrassed flush replaced the sudden panicky look on his face. Had he misjudged her or their quickly forming relationship so much that he thought she was leaving already?

He watched her with renewed longing as she walked with gently swaying hips to her large bag and rummaged through it. Picking up a lipstick case, she turned and winked at him while covering her full lips with a dark red hue.

John closed his eyes, sleepy and wonderfully content. He didn't want to make her uncomfortable by staring at her like a love-sick puppy. He heard the whisper of her bare feet on the carpet as she approached him.

John knew she stood next to the bed, for he could feel her overwhelming presence. He kept his eyes closed in childish anticipation. The thought of her leaning over to give him a sip from the wine glass, her pendulous breasts swinging freely in front of his face, made him excited again. Opening his eyes, he had a soft smile plastered on his face.

The smile stayed frozen there as he stared at Miranda's wicked expression and the hatchet she held up over her head. John's thoughts turned as crazy as the look in his lover's eyes as he focused his shocked attention on the dried brown stains splashed along the blade's smooth edge.

Miranda sat relaxed in the sagging recliner, legs propped once again over one arm. She sipped on her now flat beer and hummed a favorite melody to herself. One stiletto-heeled shoe swung idly from her toes as she gently moved her leg in time to the rhythm in her head.

"Here's to us, John." She waved the glass toward the table by the window. Getting up slowly and stretching the tiredness out of her back, she walked over to the goldfish bowl. It was a dandy all right, huge and ugly in her eyes. But she'd smiled when John had explained earlier how he'd converted the vintage piece into a special place for his one fat fish.

"Now we'll always be together." She looked lovingly down into the jar.

Miranda hadn't planned on John's head plopping down into his goldfish bowl. But neither had she known that he could be so swift. He'd caught her arm at the moment she was ready to strike with the hatchet.

Jumping up, he'd run from her. Since she couldn't catch him once he was just about to rip the front door open and escape, she'd had to make an instantaneous decision. The hatchet had flown through the air to sink inches deep into his back.

John had fallen to his knees, stunned, simply staring up at her. His action had made her angry. After tearing the weapon from John's back in a spray of blood, she'd held it like a bat and had then taken a powerful swing at his neck. It surprised even her that his head had flown through the air, spun several times, to then land with a loud *plunk* into the jar.

As his headless body thudded to the floor, blood squirting from the jagged hole to bathe the carpet in scarlet, she became even more upset. He had messed up her carefully orchestrated plan on taking him out gently. She hadn't wanted his last moment to be painful or filled with terror.

"Why did you run from me, John?"

Wham! The hatchet dug deep into his chest as she struck his body. *Whack!* The second blow split his slim abdomen and intestines spilled out. Her weapon went up and down numerous times as the rage overtook her.

After several minutes, she hung her head down, clutching her knees. She was exhausted, but satisfaction flowed through her veins, creating a lovely glowing sensation. Almost as good as an organism, but not quite.

Blood drenched her body. Wiping both hands over her abdomen, she spread the blood to areas that were spotless. Mmmm. Warm blood. Her nipples hardened and for a second she wished she hadn't killed John so quickly.

A slamming door nearby drew her attention back to the present and the jar in front of her. Miranda squealed, staring in disgust at the goldfish, which was pecking at John's flesh in the small amount of room it had left. She tapped the glass, trying to dislodge it. The fish ignored her.

Glancing around, she spotted the fishnet lying on the table behind the jar. Picking up John's discarded shirt on the couch, she used it to grip the net's handle. No use leaving fingerprints behind. Scooping up the obese, hungry goldfish, she flipped the net over, dumping the nasty thing onto the floor. It flopped and gulped. She almost giggled. John had gulped like that just before she'd taken off his head.

She knelt in front of the goldfish jar, gazing at John's frozen features intently. She loved the way he still smiled at her, even though his large eyes held a glint of fear. She shrugged. It didn't hurt for a man to fear his woman a little bit.

Miranda also loved the way his adorable hair stuck up above the water, looking like a tiny island with thin trees straggling upward. His cute little nose was pressed against the glass and she knew he longed to touch her again.

She hugged herself dreamily. He had been an inapt and inexperienced lover to begin with, but with her tutelage, he had become a wonderful partner.

Hating the feel of the blood on her hands that had now turned tacky, Miranda headed for the bathroom. She showered thoroughly, and then cleaned up the apartment, dressing only after making sure no smidgen of her presence remained. She gathered the soiled sheet from the bed and stuck it in her purse, then looked over the rooms carefully. John's body was strewn about in gory pieces and a large pool of blood had soaked into the carpet. She shrugged. There was no cleaning up that mess. Miranda never worried about leaving evidence of her kills. It was fun playing cat and mouse with the police. Besides, she had never been arrested, so her fingerprints and DNA were not on record.

Of course, the authorities would know a woman had been here and had probably perpetrated the crime, as her bloody footprints trailed from the corpse to the bathroom.

She frowned, hating the headlines she knew would be coming. ***The Praying Mantis Killer*** was a stupid name, she thought. Sure, she beheaded her lovers, but she didn't eat them! Disgusting and unimaginative news reporters.

She leaned close to the jar and kissed the glass near John's open mouth. Then she stood up and gathered her large handbag, placing the hatchet inside. Spying the discarded wine glasses, she added hers to the purse. It saved cleaning it off.

Returning her attention once again to John, she admired the way his head floated gently in its watery grave. Tiny red rivulets of blood streamed from the gaping wound and globules of jagged flesh made an unattractive neckline. Miranda shook her head. She had to remember to sharpen the edge; its dull surface had made a sloppy job of her lovely John.

She spread out the towel she used to dry herself on the floor, then got a plastic trash bag from the kitchen. Carefully, she gripped John by the hair and placed his head on the towel, wrapping it inside the terrycloth, then placed it within the trash bag.

She tucked the head away amongst the other items already stowed in her large bag.

Grimacing as she closed the door to the dreary apartment, Miranda knew John would be pleased with his new home. Her frown gave way to a wide smile as she remembered him telling her how he wished to leave one day. That he wished for his life to change.

Her thoughts quickly turned to the rearranging she'd have to do once she arrived home. There was Lewis, Barry, and Frank to consider, all long time favorites. But John deserved center stage as her newest conquest.

First, she would have to clean him up, then place his sweet head in a formaldehyde-filled jar. It was shorter and wider than the jar which had held his ugly goldfish.

With a laugh, she realized it really wasn't that much different than the goldfish jar; it was the content inside that made it so much better.

Now John would be with her forever. She adored shy men and John had been the epitome of such claim; yet he'd been a marvelous lover and was worthy of this honor.

Of course, there was also Richard, Shawn, Aaron…

THE RESERVATION

SHANE KOCH

Judith pushed the stroller along the sidewalk. The little wheels crunched fallen leaves. It was a new sidewalk, so she didn't have to pay as much attention, didn't have to worry as much about spilling her baby out because of cracks or overgrowth.

A good sidewalk for the *good* side of the street.

She glanced at the sidewalk on the other side of the street, the *bad* side, the side where the battered and cracked concrete slabs bordered the reservation. No one ever walked on the sidewalk that bordered the reservation, except kids on a dare, and even then only for a moment.

Judith stopped and brushed her breeze-whipped black hair from her eyes. She tied it back in a ponytail. She walked around to the front of the stroller and bent over to check the baby. The baby was sleeping. Judith glanced over at the reservation and noticed with revulsion that one of those *things* was leering at her. She never should have stopped to bend over anywhere near the reservation, and she didn't know what she was thinking. She should never have even walked her baby stroller down the opposite sidewalk, but her mind had wandered. The only barrier between her baby and the staring *thing* was a street and an electrified razor-wire fence. A breeze kicked up, and the thick bushes behind her swayed, newly dead leaves flittering through the air

The *thing* across the street was ruining autumn.

Judith stood and regarded the monstrosity that lasciviously eyed her body. She had a sudden vision of the creature ripping her nipples off and eating them. She saw the almond-shaped eyes, the round face, and the stubby arms that ended in chubby, grasping fingers that would eagerly violate her every orifice with retard-strengthened lust. The wet mouth on that chinless face licked its lips and Judith shivered in disgust. She looked past the mongoloid to the squat, bunker-like building in the center of the reservation, a gray box surrounded by a field of dead grass and a few dying trees.

The soldiers that ran the facility let the *things* go outside twice a day, ushering the creatures outside with cattle prods and clubs. But the guards weren't supposed the let the mongoloids get too close to the fence, because rape-lust sometimes caused the creatures to electrocute themselves by hurling their bodies into the electrified chain-links.

She noticed that the guards were watching several of the mongoloids fight over a squirrel's corpse, taking bets. Judith wondered if she could entice the *thing* watching her through the electric fence. She shook the thought from her head. She hated living near the reservation, but the property was cheap. More and more, her mind drifted to thoughts of the underground facility beneath the bunker. The pens where they kept the mongoloids. Nobody even knew how many of those *things* were down there. There could be a thousand of them, hiding in the dark, wallowing in filth, waiting. She had a morbid, obsessive curiosity about the facility, nightmares about it, and on occasion she had lurid sexual fantasies about the creatures. She'd never told anyone about the fantasies, she wasn't even sure they were fantasies, and she suspected that her mind was just punishing her for some reason. It was a lie. They were fantasies, she knew it, even though she lied to herself, trying to somehow convince herself that she was normal, she couldn't help it. Her mind was her mind, and that's all there was to it.

Judith glanced around to see no one on the street. She looked the *thing* in the face and slowly licked her lips. Turning, she bent over to check the baby again, keeping her knees locked and her ass in the air. She looked back, past her thigh. The *thing* was rubbing its crotch and Judith realized that she didn't even know if the creature was male or female. Judith was getting wet, too. She stood up quickly and went back to pushing her stroller towards home. She felt a little shame. She couldn't tell if she felt bad because she had tried to trick the mongoloid into electrocuting itself, or if she was ashamed that she had stopped. Certainly, she didn't have sympathy for the *thing*; did she? No. In her most sickening fantasies, she might have used one of them as a warm sex toy, but she didn't care if their entire accursed race died out.

Fuck them.

The mongoloid walked along the fence as far as it could go before the reservation property ended. It watched Judith walk away, and it rubbed its crotch— then it orgasmed.

Hours later, at dinner, while Judith and her family prepared to eat, the dining room window suddenly exploded inward as that very mongoloid she'd tempted earlier came bursting in with enough force to flail onto the dining room table like an electrified Mexican jumping bean covered in shards of glass. In its mad gyrations, the *thing's* foot whipped out and kicked the baby in the face, killing it instantly. Judith and her husband, Mike, jumped to their feet as the creature found its footing among the toppled shakers, smeared casserole and spilled lemonade.

The *thing*, of course, was naked. As Judith snatched up the baby from the floor, she noticed the huge penis dangling between the mongoloid's pasty thighs. She backed away, clutching her dead infant, and screamed.

The *thing* smiled at her, and Judith knew what it was going to do with that horse-like dick. Mike grabbed a knife from the table and stabbed the mongoloid in the back. The *thing* screeched with an inhuman fury.

Judith awoke with a start. She was on the living room couch, the television's haze casting a ghostly light. She looked immediately to the playpen. The baby was sleeping.

Mike, in his favorite chair reading a magazine, looked up. "Bad dream?" he asked with a smile.

"Shit," Judith said, as she shook the cobwebs from her head.

He put his magazine aside, interested. "What was it?"

"That goddamned reservation," she sighed. "I was daydreaming, and I accidentally passed by it today when I was walking the baby."

"Did they have those *things* outside?"

"Yes, and one of them was by the fence, watching me. And it was touching itself."

"Was that what the dream was about?"

She looked at the baby. "No. We were eating in the dining room and it jumped through the window and killed the baby. It was naked."

Mike laughed and sat back with his magazine. "Jesus, was it a boy mongoloid or a girl one?"

Judith looked at Mike, annoyed at being laughed at. "A boy mongoloid," she said with a tone. "Its dick was way bigger than yours."

"Then it must have been a dream," he teased. "Maybe we can arrange a visit to the reservation for you. You can meet your new boyfriend."

Judith rolled her eyes and fell back onto the couch. "Fuck you," she sighed. "It was a bad dream. It killed our baby."

Mike absently motioned to the playpen. "Our baby's not dead. Just stay away from the reservation from now on, all right? Last thing we need is to get fined because one of those dumb fucks electrocutes itself trying to get at your ass."

Judith glanced at him. She wondered what Mike would think if he knew she had actually tried to get that *thing* to electrocute itself. She would never tell him, of course, but she fantasized about telling him. She dreamed that her attempted murder of one of those rotten retards would first disgust Mike, but then get him rock hard. Then he'd hate-fuck her on the kitchen table. She smiled and drifted off to sleep again.

Later, Judith woke up to silence. The house was dark and quiet. She realized that Mike had left her sleeping on the couch and had gone to bed without her. She glanced sleepily at the empty playpen. Heavy-footed, she walked up the stairs and drifted into the baby's room. The baby was sleeping quietly, and she checked to make sure her little angel was alive, always dreading that the baby would be dead and it would somehow be her fault because she was a bad mother. The baby was fine.

She looked around the baby's room, the weak moonlight struggling sickly through the sheer curtains, the crib's bars casting deep shadow grooves on the colorless carpet. She was an okay mother, right? The baby had everything that was needed. She was nice to the baby. She even thought she might love the baby. Judith shook her head and sighed. Of course she loved her baby, and she almost laughed. Who wouldn't love their baby?

She made sure the baby was alive again and then shuffled to her bedroom. Mike was asleep. She thought about going under the covers and sucking him awake like she used to, but it was too much trouble. She wondered what the sexless mongoloid was doing. Was it fucking something? She slinked into bed and she drifted off again to sleep.

Mike was gone when she woke up. He'd gone to work and he didn't wake her. She got up and checked on the baby. It was asleep still, alive.

Judith went to the bathroom in her burgeoning wakefulness, took off her clothes, and sat on the toilet. While she did nature's business, she thought of how much she didn't really like Mike all that much. She got up and turned around to look into the bowl, once again repressing the urge to touch her own feces, to squish it in her fingers. She wiped, flushed, and took a shower.

After months of work, she'd finally gotten her body back after the baby. She was only a little fleshy in all the right places, but the rest of her was tight, and she washed slowly, enjoying her body. She thought about making herself orgasm while she showered, but decided not to because it was usually a chore when she did it to herself. She needed someone else to do stuff to her, on her, in her, for it to be really good. She needed to be used by someone, or she needed to use someone to really flow.

Then she remembered the mongoloid. When she'd teased that mongoloid, it made her wet instantly, and she knew that even though she shouldn't, she was going to do it again, or at least try. She contracted slightly and she cooed to herself while she washed her hard, soft body. Yes, she would tease the mongoloid again, and her hands worked a little extra time while she showered.

She dried herself and brushed her teeth. Looking at herself in the mirror while she brushed, she gazed into her eyes, and she didn't really know what was there behind those green saucers. She rinsed her mouth out just as the baby started to cry. It was hungry. Naked, Judith breezed through the house, ignoring the baby, and walked down to the kitchen. She picked up the little electric pump, and each in turn, pumped her heavy breasts impatiently, slowly filling the pump reservoir with milk. She watched the machine suck at her nipple with a slight grimace. This was something she *had to do,* and she pretended that she didn't resent it. Well, maybe she didn't *have* to do it, but it was what Mike and her parents expected her to do, because it was supposed to be better for the baby or some nonsense, and she always did what she was supposed to do.

She pulled the pump from her breast with a little suction noise. The thought came to her to spit in the milk, but she squashed it. Her mind was a mess sometimes, and it understood her and her impulse control problems better than she did. But it *was* her mind after all, right?

She fed and changed the baby and she put her child in the playpen. She always appreciated the economy of her baby's crying habits. Her baby only cried when wanting something. Once that need was filled, the baby was quiet, almost contemplative. It was good that way.

Judith remembered that she was naked. She'd been naked all morning, which was too long. She never thought of herself as *nude.* She was naked when she wasn't wearing clothes, and when she was naked long enough, she would start thinking about it, and that would make her tingly.

It was time to get dressed and go for her walk.

It was cold outside, so she had an excuse to wear a long coat. She put on her purple coat, the one that reached her knees and buttoned all the way down. She put on tennis shoes and pulled her hair back into a pony tail. She went back to the bathroom and quickly put on her outside face, with just enough makeup to look like she wasn't wearing any at all.

She gathered and dressed the baby for a walk outside, then put her child in the stroller. She left the house, rolling the stroller down the driveway, and the cold air crept and crawled up her legs and under her coat, pinching at her naked body with chilly fingers. Houses and yards called to her as she walked. She often wondered what was going on in those houses, picturing the filthy and odd habits people engaged in when they were alone. She knew that someone in one of the houses she passed was probably up to something that she would want to watch. She nodded at any neighbors she saw, minded the stroller, and walked slowly, excited with her secret nakedness.

The closer she got to the reservation, the faster her heart pounded. She could feel herself getting wet and was surprised by it again, and her head started to swim a little with a kind of anticipatory sexual panic.

The reservation loomed ever closer, and Judith was starting to worry that her wetness would begin to run down her thigh. It didn't, but she imagined that she was toting a water balloon fit to bursting inside her. Whatever was regular about her was floating away and becoming blind, and the puppet strings of her secret mind now manipulated and pulled at her.

Judith rounded the corner on the bad stretch of sidewalk across from the reservation, and the mongoloid was there. Judith's breath turned shallow and her legs felt rubbery. Of course it was there, the sexless *thing*, and it was all so horribly perfect. Her intentions must have been like a dog whistle to the *thing*. It *knew*, and it was waiting for her.

She stopped for a moment and let out a shivering sigh through trembling lips. She was sexually teasing a pathetic animal in the middle of the street, trying to entice it to death, while in the company of her baby. And it was the best feeling in the world. She surrendered to it and abandoned whatever was right or wrong for the sake of the moment, for her loosening, popping pussy, for madness. On unsteady legs she walked to the bushes, directly across the street from the mongoloid.

The mongoloid watched expectantly, and behind it, its fellow creatures shuffled and fought on the dying and patchy grass of the compound before the plain concrete bunker.

The only guard Judith could see was in the distance, leaning on a bunker wall, and facing the other way. There was no one else anywhere. She looked at the mongoloid and her heart felt like it was about to explode, and her eyelids fluttered as she drew a breath through her teeth.

She smiled at the creature and slowly ran her hands up and down her purple coat. The mongoloid's hand moved to its crotch and it started to rub. Judith looked around again but the street was empty.

She undid the button closest to her crotch and spread the coat open in a diamond-shaped flash. She showed the mongoloid her perfectly trimmed bush and Judith positively buzzed as she reached inside and rubbed her straining clit. She knew she was going to orgasm.

Her free hand exposed one of her breasts, and she roughly tweaked her nipple while she leaned against the stroller. But it wasn't enough. She fell to her knees as her hand frantically worked between her legs.

She gave in completely and sat on the sidewalk, throwing her legs apart, and popping the lowest button on her coat, she spread her legs wide while she masturbated for the mongoloid, showing the creature everything she had to show. She nudged the stroller from behind and it rolled a couple inches, the baby asleep.

The mongoloid's jaw dropped open and it made a surprised grunt at the sight of a human vagina ferociously spread and being wetly worked. The creature uttered a guttural groan and it hurled itself into the electric fence.

The current froze the animal into a death grip on the chain-links, its face twisted in pain and confusion as it was electrocuted.

The mongoloid twisted and convulsed and burned, as it died watching Judith orgasm on the sidewalk across the street.

She watched it die and then got to her feet, fixing her clothes while still in the throws of her orgasm, She continued to cum in lessening waves as she quickly pushed the stroller away on unsure and shaky legs, hoping in panic that no one would notice the wet spot on the seat of her coat that she knew was probably there.

Several other mongoloids watched her go as the guards finally noticed the burning corpse on the electric fence.

Judith had orgasmed ridiculously hard, but she wished she could have taken her time, wished it had lasted longer. She distanced herself from the reservation, pushing the stroller quickly through the cold. Her crotch and legs were cold now. She was cold. She realized in horror the danger of what she'd just done. She could have been seen.

It would be impossible to explain what she'd done. She wouldn't get into that much trouble, but people would think she was a pervert or crazy. Correction: they would *find out* that she was perverted or crazy. She hadn't seen any cameras. Did they have them? She was almost sure that they must have security cameras at the reservation. They would have seen her. She knew it, and her family wouldn't understand and they wouldn't want anything to do with her after this.

She heard an alarm in the distance. It was behind her, at the reservation. She glanced over her shoulder and from around the corner that lead to the complex came loping three mongoloids. They were coming after her.

Her eyes widened in shock. She knew immediately that the *thing* she had tricked to death had shorted out the electric fence. The creatures were escaping! She heard gunshots in the distance and the three mongoloids were running toward her.

"This is big trouble!" she said to herself. Judith grabbed the baby out of the stroller and ran as fast as she could. The baby started to cry.

Judith ran for her life, and didn't look back until she reached her house. More gunshots sounded in the distance and she heard screams, too. The three mongoloids were almost at her front lawn, their misshapen heads determined and set, their retarded eyes flashing with lust and murder. She unlocked her front door, threw it open, and slammed it closed just as the mongoloids reached it, throwing their bodies into it, pounding on it.

The metal mail slot lid slapped open and closed with each impact. Judith dashed up the stairs to her bedroom, slammed the door closed, and locked it. She heard the front door break open and then the breaking and overturning of furniture downstairs.

She nodded her head, took the baby to the master bathroom off the bedroom, then closed the door after putting her crying child on the floor.

She went back into the bedroom.

The *things* were on the stairs.

Judith got Mike's shotgun out of the closet. It was loaded with five shells, and she pumped one into the chamber. She aimed the shotgun at her bedroom door and waited. She knew that she'd brought this on herself, but she'd be damned if she was going to let those three fucks kill her and her baby.

She wondered just how many of her neighbors were being raped or murdered at that moment, and how she'd been the engineer of it all.

She felt strangely excited, exhilarated even, and realized again that she would never be a normal human as her mind thought for a moment about letting the mongoloids rape her to death.

She laughed wildly as the *things* broke through the bedroom door.

ABOUT THE WRITERS

Terry Alexander and his wife Phyllis live on a small farm near Porum, Oklahoma. They have 3 children and 9 grandchildren. He's a member of the Oklahoma Writers Federation, Ozark Writers League, The Arkansas Ridge Writers and The Fictioneers. Primarily a horror writer, he's been published in several anthologies from Open Casket Press, Living Dead Press, Knightwatch Press, Paper Cut Publishing, Moonstone Books Pro Se Press and Mini Komix.

David H. Donaghe lives and works in the high desert of Southern California with his wife and family. He has three passions in life: reading, writing and riding his motorcycle. He has several short stories published in anthologies by Living Dead Press. His short story collection, Monroe's Paranormal Investigations, is also published by Living Dead Press. His novel "Tale Spinner" was released in 2011 by Otherworld Publications. His new biker fiction novel, "Thunder Road" was released by Black Rose Writing on in 2012. He invites you to follow his blog at Dave's Blog Page, to check out his author web page at http://dhdonaghe.weebly.com/index.html and to follow him on Face Book, and Twitter. He loves hearing from his readers. You can contact him by email at davidhdonaghe@yahoo.com He's currently enjoying life on the high desert while working on his next novel.

Anthony Giangregorio is the author of 45 novels, most about zombies, and has edited over 50 anthologies and novels. His work has appeared in Dead Science & Metahumans vs. the Undead by Coscomentertainment, Dead Worlds: Undead Stories Volumes 1-7, and Wolves of War by Library of the Living Dead Press. He also has stories in End of Days: An Apocalyptic Anthology Vol. 1-5, the Book of the Dead series Vol. 1-6 by LDP, Zombie Zoology by Severed Press, and two anthologies with Pill Hill Press. He's also the creator of the ten book action/zombie series titled Deadwater and the apocalyptic series Warriors of the Apocalypse. His action/horror novel Dead Rage is being optioned for a movie at this time.

Samuel J. Guss is working towards a degree in History, with a special focus on apocalyptic events and how they changed social behavior. In the meantime he writes, plays war games, works and takes lot of photographs, especially at weddings.

You can keep up to date with his work at http://samuelguss.com

Chauma Smith Guss lives and works in Birmingham Alabama, and will tell you about her dogs if given any opportunity. She is a not-so-closet fan of horror and dark urban fantasy, serial killer trivia, and her husband Sam.

While watching the news for evidence of zombie outbreaks is a fun game, she is the only actual true believer in the family. She can be found late at night reading post-apocalyptic fiction of all sorts with the covers pulled over her head and the machete within reach. Outside her passion for reading and writing, her hobbies include speaking at church, teaching Sunday School, and participating in a wedding ministry. No, really.

Julie R. Kendrick is an English author living in Northhamptonshire. She writes horror and dark fantasy. Her stories have been published in various US and UK anthologies. She's currently working on her first novel.

Shane Koch is the author of "Weathering Your Reanimation: Tips for 'Surviving' Your Existence as a Zombie," and the forthcoming "Your Mongoloid."

Daniel Loubier is a relative up-and-comer in the horror genre. "Island Getaway" is the author's second publication under Open Casket Press. His zombie short, "A Family Tradition," was included in, "Dead Christmas: A Zombie Anthology" (Fall 2011).

His work has also been featured on www.BrutalasHell.com, as part of their short fiction web series. Loubier's first novel, "Dead Summit," a zombie horror, was released in October, 2011. Visit him on Facebook (Daniel Loubier), Twitter (@DeadSummit), and on his website, www.danloubier.com

Christopher Nadeau is the author of "Dreamers at Infinity's Core" and has over two dozen published short stories in such august publications as The Horror Zine, Sci-Fi Short Story Magazine, Ghostlight Magazine and many more. He was interviewed as part of Suspense Radio's up and coming authors program and collaborated on two "machinima" films with UK animator Celestial Elf called "The Gift," and 'The Deerhunter's Tale," both of which can be viewed on YouTube. His novel "Echoes of Infinity's Core" is slated for a 2012 release. An active member of the Great Lakes Association of Horror Writers, he resides in Southeastern Michigan with his wife Lorie and two petulant long-hair Chihuahuas.

Wayne C. Rogers is a resident of Las Vegas. He's written one book, "The House of Blood," which is an erotic/horror novel and just about as kinky as you can get. He's presently turning his horror novellas of "The Tunnels" and "The Encounter" into a long novel, and has two written screenplays based on them out there for those with a few bucks to invest in making a film.

Marc Shemmans is a writer from Birmingham, UK who has had several stories published in a variety of magazines and anthologies from both sides of the Atlantic. He's hoping they will find homes as soon as they're finished.

John Skerchock's professional work came first in the form of an article for Fantaco then with a horror story for Twilight Zone's sister magazine Night Cry. Work then followed with Druktenis Publishing, Horror Biz, Chiller Theatre and several websites. John also produced the classic Zacherley Scrapbook.

M.L. Traxler grew up watching old horror classics, so it's a life-long love. Stephen King & Dean Koontz were read with pleasure, as well as many other horror writers. She's been on a zombie reading kick the last two years and is a huge fan of "The Walking Dead." This is her 1st published story for horror, and she hopes fans will enjoy her expansion into writing this genre. She is also a well-known romance author using the pen name Myra Nour. See her other works at: www.myranour.net

DEADLY HUNT
by Mariah Deitrick

When extreme hunt enthusiast, Drake Marshal, began his career as a hired hunter, he had no idea he would one day become the prey. If he had, he never would have found himself running for his life in a zombie-infested jungle.

Will Drake's years of hunting experience be enough to keep him alive? Or will he let his sympathy for others get him killed.

ZOMBIE TALES
Edited by Anthony Giangregorio and Vincenzo Bilof

The earth cannot contain the dead, graves opening wide to disgorge rotting bodies!

Maggot-filled, bloated with dripping pus, these mindless creatures only have one need—to feed on human flesh!

The zombie lives again in this anthology, filled with hungry corpses that can't get enough. Death, despair and loss, all will be experienced as you are taken on a trip into the very bowels of Hell.

The living dead are not forgiving, nor do they feel pity.

As you feel their cold embrace, and their teeth sinking into your throat to tear out your jugular, just pray it's a quick death, before oblivion claims you.

THE FALL OF PITTSBURGH
A Zombie Novel
by Matt Demas

Living at an imprisonment school is hard enough without the walking dead trying to eat you every second of the day.

Keith Merth and his classmates are forced into conducting experiments on things better left alone. Soon, the students begin to act out of the ordinary, many downright irrationally.

And it seems one of the main side effects of the experiments is that the student body has turned into zombies with a taste for human flesh!

Will Keith and his friends make it out alive? Or will they become a warm meal for the living dead.

ZOMBIES, MONSTERS, CREATURES OF THE NIGHT

OPEN CASKET PRESS

OPEN CASKET PRESS.COM

THE NEW NAME IN HORROR

THE PLACE TO GO FOR ZOMBIE AND APOCALYPTIC FICTION

LIVING DEAD PRESS

WHERE THE DEAD WALK

www.livingdeadpress.com

ZOMBIE AND APOCALYPTIC FICTION AT IT'S BEST!

OPEN CASKET PRESS.COM
LIVING DEAD PRESS.COM

VICTORY OF THE DEAD
ANTHONY GIANGREGORIO

www.ingramcontent.com/pod-product-compliance
Lightning Source LLC
Chambersburg PA
CBHW070501120726
47910CB00003B/1082